THE CHESS MASTER'S VIOLIN

Jennifer Willows

✻ PUBLISHER'S NOTE

Some would call it serendipity, coincidence, or karma, but others (including me) would call it a God thing.

On March 27 of this year (2011), I received an email from Jennifer Willows with a submission for our *America's Got Stories* short story contest. I took a quick look as I usually did to get an idea of the flavor and quality of the story and to make sure it met the requirements, which included a limitation of no fewer than 1,000 and no more than 2,500 words.

Apparently, young Miss Willows had misread the upper limit as her story was 25,000 words long, far in excess of the limit but wonderfully crafted and beautifully written.

I called her, and we laughed about her fortunate mistake. I told her, "Your story's a bit long for a short story, and not long enough for a novel. But if you're willing to finish it, we would publish it."

She agreed, and we signed her on the spot. She worked with two of our editors, Donna Levy and Rose Bethard, to establish her voice and make some changes so the story would flow better. Then she set sail and wrote her way home to this book, her first of what I expect will be many wonderful God things in her life.

John Köehler, September 2011

The Chess Master's Violin

Jennifer Willows

NEW YORK

VIRGINIA

THE CHESS MASTER'S VIOLIN

by Jennifer Willows

© Copyright 2011 by Andrea Coler

ISBN 978-1-938467-08-0

Edited by Rose Bethard
Text design by Marshall McClure
Cover design by John Köehler

Published by

an imprint of Morgan James Publishing

5 Penn Plaza, 23rd floor
c/o Morgan James Publishing
New York, NY 10001
212-574-7939
www.koehlerbooks.com

Publisher
John Köehler

Executive Editor
Joe Coccaro

❋ TABLE OF CONTENTS

❋ ACKNOWLEDGEMENTS

First and foremost, God deserves all the credit for this book. A few months ago, I misread a word count, and now I'm getting a book published. It is only by His grace that it was at all possible.

Next, I would like to thank both Donna Levy and Rose Bethard for their amazing editing abilities and patience. Donna started me out, and Rose was there to help me finish. Together, you two helped me create my story, and I will always be grateful. Thank you!

Dear John (I've been waiting to say that), thanks for giving me a chance. You took a big risk by taking on my book, and I appreciate that. Thank you, oh wise Master Publisher.

Lastly, thank you Andrea Waldrop for all of your help and inspiration. You are my art and literary critic in addition to being my best friend (which is tough enough). ¡Gracias chica!

Jennifer Willows

❄ INTRODUCTION

"It is I who should be thanking you, for it seems as though you have saved my life many times." He paused and pulled a small parcel out of his pocket. "No English gentleman should be without one of these, and I hope you will accept it as a small token of my gratitude."

I opened the small parcel and discovered a beautiful silver pocket watch inside complete with a chain. My initials were engraved on the front cover and on the inside of the lid was an engraving of a pair of eyes—identical to those on the tablets. I looked up quickly, but Hawkins was gone. I thought I could pick him out near the exit, but there were so many people that I couldn't be sure. I put the watch into my waistcoat pocket and looped the chain through a buttonhole. It was an item I would treasure for the rest of my life.

"To Paris, my husband," Agatha said when I had joined her on the train.

"Let's get going, my dearest. We have our entire lives ahead of us now."

✳ CHAPTER I

T HERE ARE COUNTLESS STORIES IN THE
world with many themes. Some stories tell the great
adventures of brave heroes, a few speak of the clash between gods
and men, and others simply chronicle the lives of lonely souls
whose greatest quest is to make it through each day.

The story I want to tell you is true, though it is difficult to
believe. It doesn't tell of a great warrior who goes into a noble
battle. There are no dragons to slay in this book, but dragons don't
always come shaped like the lizard creatures of fairy tales. Perhaps
we all have our own dragons that we must slay throughout our
lifetime, if we will only be brave enough to ride out in conquest.
This is the tale of how I defeated a few dragons in my life. I
learned to overcome the word impossible. In the process, I found
my true friends and where I truly belonged.

My name is Andrew M. Collins, Ph.D. I was born in Olympia,
Washington, USA on September 1, 1981. I have always been the
restless sort and find it difficult to remain anywhere for very long.
I suppose I was always trying to find some place where I fit in, but
it took me years to arrive there. After graduating high school, I
attended a local undergraduate school and switched majors about
five times before settling on psychology. The terrors of the human
mind fascinated me, and I believed that more often than not

medication was not the answer. I wanted to try to help hurting people if I could, so I earned my bachelor's degree and moved to Boston to pursue a master's degree. I ended up going the full distance and received a doctorate degree specializing in social psychology.

School was difficult, and I thought that afterward life would be easy. I was mistaken. After I graduated, I barely had a nickel to my name and no real friends. I stayed in Boston, living off part-time jobs at whatever fast-food joints would hire me, but I felt lonely and stuck. I concluded that if I didn't get away I would be trapped for the rest of my life, so I called my brother for help.

Richard—my older brother and only living family member—is almost completely opposite me. I was a shy, a somewhat timid child, but he was bold, daring, and confident. In high school he was the perfect model of a popular jock, and I was the nerd with glasses. I always looked up to him, though, and he protected me from my peers. However, once he graduated, I was on my own, and high school became a veritable hell for me.

Richard was expected to become a legend among athletes, but an unfortunate injury dashed his dreams. Not sure what else to do, he fell back on his second love, writing, and became a successful journalist. After earning an associate's degree in journalism from the local community college he began writing for *The Olympian* and is a published author besides. Along the way, he got married, bought a house in Tenino, and had two lovely daughters. He is quite content with his life—a state of mind I thought I would never achieve—and found huge success, although no great distinction.

Richard was sympathetic when I called him. He offered me the spare bedroom at his house for as long as I needed. He also paid for a plane ticket and promised to be at the airport to pick me up when I arrived. A few days later, I was sitting in a plane, courtesy of Delta Airlines, flying west toward Seattle.

I was relieved when the plane ride finally ended, for I am rather afraid of heights. Every time the plane jarred, I was sure we were going down. I had the misfortune to sit between a thin woman who sat quietly with a book and a large man who made it his mission to scare me to death by telling horror stories of airplane crashes. We finally landed, safely, around 7:30 p.m. I had no trouble collecting my bags, but the man who had sat next to me wasn't so lucky. Despite the trials he put me through, I felt sorry for him, but there was nothing I could do to help.

Although I could still recall painful memories from the past, upon arriving in western Washington, I had great hopes that life would be better for me. There is great power to be had in positive thinking, and I resolved to remain optimistic no matter what happened. After all, I had escaped Boston and a whole new life lay before me. This was my beginning.

I strode through the lobby, heading toward the door, and allowed myself a slight feeling of pride as I raised my eyes from the floor. Unfortunately, a janitor had recently mopped the lobby, and I was the only person who didn't notice the sign: Caution: Wet Floor. I slipped, nearly did a front flip, and landed prostrate on the floor. I sat up with a bleeding gash on my forehead, and tried hard to fight off the pessimism that threatened to overwhelm me. A man in a business suit asked if I was alright, but I waved him off in embarrassment. Thus, the prodigal son returned to Washington, only to be beaten by a wet floor.

The airport staff was extremely apologetic about the incident and offered to call an ambulance. I declined and just asked for a towel and an ice pack. They were, no doubt, fearful of a lawsuit, but I didn't think it fair to sue them for my own negligence. I was sure they all thought me an idiot, and I groaned inwardly to think that they would be telling this story for months to come.

I found a chair in the lobby and sat down in dejection. Richard appeared to be running late, and I had already managed to humiliate myself publicly. I began to wonder if it wouldn't be better just to go back to Boston, or somewhere even more remote, when a familiar voice drew me from my troubled thoughts.

"Andrew?"

I looked up and found myself staring into a face that could have easily been my own, except for the mustache and beard.

"Richard!! Man, am I glad to see you!"

"I'll bet! Sorry I'm late. There was an accident on I-5. Traffic on the freeway is always bad, but accidents don't make it any better. What happened to your head?"

"I slipped in the lobby. I don't have a concussion or anything like that. It's just a gash."

"Ha, ha, ha! Well then, Mr. Dr. Andrew Collins, I recommend that you look before you leap next time." He hadn't changed a bit.

Traffic leaving SeaTac Airport wasn't as bad as the traffic headed there, and we sped through our nearly empty southbound lane. I looked at the congested northbound side with a feeling of pity, but Richard laughed heartily.

"Ha! Suckers!" He exclaimed.

"That's kind of rude you know." I said.

"Nah, they'd think the same thing if they were us."

"That's not the point."

"Oh, who cares?"

I shook my head and sighed. There was no point in trying to reason with him, and I quickly changed the subject. The car ride went quickly. Richard kept up a steady stream of conversation. By the time we got off the freeway in Tumwater I was well versed in the events of the past few years.

"Hey, Richard, when did they change Airdustrial Way to Tumwater Boulevard?" I asked when he paused for breath.

"Oh, a few years back. I think it was 2003, but I could be wrong. We still call it Airdustrial just to be rebellious, though."

"Ah."

This street name wasn't the only thing that had changed since my absence. The construction that had been started before I left was completed. There were many more state buildings than there used to be, and Tumwater had a crowded, modern look to it. This wasn't turning out to be the western Washington I had remembered.

We finally arrived in the dubious little town of Tenino, and I found that while Tumwater had changed, Tenino was practically the same. The two bars on Sussex Avenue were still right next to each other, the chocolate store still neighbored a denture clinic, and Scotty B's restaurant was still way too expensive. Richard's house, which was along the main road, boasted two stories with a modest yard in the back and a large oak tree in front. It was by no means extravagant, but it was comfortable. I was greeted warmly by my sister-in-law, Lisa, and two nieces, who had stayed up in anticipation of my arrival. I had only seen pictures of these two wonderful children, and it was odd to think that I was an uncle. The oldest, Katie, was eight. Her sister, Marissa, was five. Because it was a school night, they were sent to bed as soon as they had said hello.

"Well, Richard, it looks like you've done pretty well these past years," I said once the three of us were seated in the living room.

"Yup, we're pretty happy here," Richard replied with a smile. "You should really think about getting a wife of your own one of these days and settling down. It does a man good." Lisa was sitting in the chair next to him, and he squeezed her hand fondly.

"Yeah, I've thought about it, but I just don't think any woman would go for me."

"Nonsense!" Lisa protested. "You're young, smart, and almost as good looking as Richard." Richard and I both laughed at this. "I bet it won't be long before you find a girl that sweeps you off your feet."

"Nah. I'm just too old fashioned. Not to mention the fact that I'm totally technologically challenged. I mean, I don't even own a cell phone."

"You know what your problem is, Andrew?" Richard asked. "You expect too much, and you always have. Home wasn't good enough, so you left. Basic college education wasn't enough, so you became a doctor. You see what I mean? It's like you're running or something. Just settle down and be content, ok?"

"I've tried. I'm not like you, Richard. I feel there's something more for me. I just have to find it. You found your calling, but I can't seem to make up my mind what mine is."

"I'm sure you'll figure it out eventually," Lisa said.

"I hope so." I went to bed soon after this conversation, knowing that Richard was right, but wishing that Lisa was too.

MY DAYS SPENT in Tenino were pleasant ones. After being in school for so long, working hard to earn my doctorate, it was nice to slow down a bit. Summer was just commencing—as best it can in Washington—and the weather remained uncharacteristically temperate although incredibly humid. I spent most of my time on long walks among the green landscape and enjoyed catching up on my artwork. You see, while my brother is the writer, I consider myself the artist. If I had been unsuccessful in school pursuing psychology, I probably would have enrolled in an art school. It isn't my first love, but it's a nice hobby. I especially loved to paint anything in nature, particularly the fir trees and woods in our area.

My brother isn't the most active man in the world, but he enjoys the outdoors and regularly took all of us camping. We usually stayed close by for a weekend trip, but once, on a whim, we went down to Estacada, Oregon. We occasionally fished at Offutt Lake. However, I despise fish of any sort and usually throw back anything I catch. When the Fourth of July came around, Lisa proved that she could out-barbeque Richard any day, but Richard beat her when it came to desserts. I was full after dinner and lay on the grass in the backyard, a niece on either side, and watched the fireworks light up the evening sky. Although it was an idyllic moment and I had so much to be thankful for, there was still something missing. I knew deep down inside that I would have to move on again and seek contentment elsewhere.

On the afternoon of August 20, the sun shone invitingly on the warm ground, and the abundant evergreens gave off a spicy aroma. The idea of a walk was more appealing than the book I was reading. I donned hiking shorts, boots, and a t-shirt, completing the look with my favorite cowboy hat, and headed out to seek adventure. Richard and Lisa were sitting on the front porch when I stepped outside, and the girls were drawing chalk figures on the walkway.

"Uncle Andy!" Katy shouted gleefully, and Marissa giggled. I had the feeling that I was the object of a conspiracy.

"Hello there you two flowers! What's up?" I knelt down on the sidewalk.

"See my picture?" Katy pointed proudly to a scribble she had recently completed.

It was a dilapidated stick figure with a lab coat on, meant to be me. They didn't quite understand what a psychologist was, so Richard had told them I was a doctor. "Oh, it's lovely! An exact picture if I do say so myself. You're turning out to be quite an artist!" Katy blushed, and Marissa burst out into laughter. I stood up, feeling satisfied for having pleased my young nieces and headed for the front gate.

"Are you going for a walk, Andrew?" Richard queried from the porch.

"Yeah, just a short one. You want to come?"

"Nah, I'm too lazy for that. If you aren't back too late we should go fishing before it gets dark."

"Sounds good. See you all later!" I paused to take in the scene—for a happy family is somewhat difficult to find. Although I longed to be a part of this picture, I didn't fit in it. I turned away and set out to explore the unknown.

Just outside of Tenino beyond the train tracks, there is a forest of sorts, and I decided to investigate it. As I walked through the dense trees, I came upon a once well-traveled path—most likely a deer trail. I followed it for awhile, even though I expected it to disappear after a short distance. After twenty minutes of brisk walking, the path became clearer instead of more obscure, which intrigued me. I hurried along. After another half hour, the path ended in a rather mysterious clearing.

I didn't like this clearing. Although it looked like a typical clearing, it was ominous. I was sure that something terrible would happen if I entered it. I stood at the edge, watching the insects fly lazily in the dim light, chastising my cowardice, when I noticed something embedded in the dirt at the center of the clearing. From my vantage point, it looked like a stone slab, but I couldn't discern anything else about it. Curious, I slowly walked toward it.

It was a rectangular stone about a foot long by half a foot wide made of something like marble. It looked like one of those headstones that lie horizontal on a grave. I knelt in the mossy grass to brush away the debris and saw that it had an inscription and drawings. The tablet was engraved with a curious pair of eyes, words below the eyes, and vines that decorated the edges. The eyes held me transfixed. To my astonishment, the engravings started to glow with an eerie bluish light. I was frightened but couldn't draw myself away. The eyes flashed blindingly, and a force hurled me backward.

For a few seconds, I felt as though I was falling, spinning, and floating all at the same time in every direction—and then I blacked out. When I woke up, the clearing was gone, and I wasn't in Tenino anymore.

❋ CHAPTER II

WHERE THERE SHOULD HAVE BEEN trees, I saw buildings. Disoriented, dizzy, and nauseated, I was forced to close my eyes until the sensation passed. Once I recovered, I sat up slowly, trying to process what I was seeing and why I was seeing it. I was in the center of a dirt lane with patches of grass on either side, large brick buildings, and an old church with a small cemetery, and it was a beautiful day—wherever it was. I thought I might be lying behind the row of the old-style buildings that line Sussex Avenue in Tenino, but then I noticed the people.

There weren't many pedestrians on the lane, but they grabbed my attention. Although it was warm out, the women wore long dresses that completely covered their arms and went up their necks and had hats adorned with feathers. The men wore dark pants, frock coats, top hats, and gloves and carried canes. As they passed me, they whispered to each other and moved to the other side of the lane to avoid me. I stared at them with open mouth and complete wonder.

I stood up. My mind raced with questions, and my head spun in shock. How could this be possible? It was far too real to be a dream, and yet, how could it be reality? I had been in Tenino just a few minutes ago, but now I had no idea where I was. Every possible and impossible solution went through my head. Was I dead? No, I still had a pulse. Was I hallucinating? This was unlikely, although not impossible. Maybe it was a dream after all.

A gentleman in a top hat approached me and asked if I was alright. My panic got the better of me. I screamed in the man's face, and ran blindly down the lane as fast as I could while people scattered out of my way.

Thinking back on it now, my cheeks turn red with embarrassment. I must have been a sight in my shorts, boots, t-shirt, and cowboy hat, running down the street like a crazed maniac. I sprinted around a corner and straight into what felt like a wall, but was a man—a small man. Despite his size, he withstood the force of me colliding with him. I stared into his remarkably blue eyes—before passing out.

I WOKE UP A FEW HOURS LATER and found myself lying on a couch in an untidy room. A desk was about fifteen feet in front of me and littered with papers. It was situated directly between two windows that faced out into the street. On the wall to the left of the desk was a bureau stuffed with papers. Next to the bureau was the fireplace. The mantelpiece was littered with scraps of paper, knives, ink pens, and various other oddities. Opposite the fireplace was a large bookshelf. Next to it stood a small table that I later learned to call a sideboard. The sideboard had some books on it, as well as a scarf and a pair of gloves. In front of the bookshelf was a round table with a dirty plate on it. There were two doors behind me, with a lamp sitting on a table between them. The door closest to the fireplace was set back a few feet more than the other, which left room for some paintings on the wall. Directly in front of me were two armchairs that faced the doors. Nestled in the armchair closest to the fire was a violin —the only object in the entire room that seemed to be treated with care.

My head throbbed, and I was dazed as I looked around. The room was lit only by the fire in the fireplace and the dim lamp on the table behind me. The room seemed eerie with odd shadows.

There were various pictures on the beige-colored walls, most of which were sketches that had been framed and hung. One was of a woman with terrifying eyes that peered at me as she stretched her scrawny hand out. A log in the fireplace cracked, and I jumped, startled by the sound.

I decided to see if my legs would still work and stood up slowly. Whoever had brought me here had changed me into to a long, dress-like garment. My clothes were neatly folded on the chair next to the couch, with my boots placed on top of the pile. As I stood thinking, the door was thrown open violently by the man I had bumped into during my wild flight. He didn't say a word to me but dashed straight for the desk with an envelope in his hand. He sat down, tore open the envelope, and quickly read the contents. With an exclamation of disgust, he tore the letter up and sank back into his chair as if all of his energy had been consumed. When he made no sign that he was going to move, I decided to introduce myself. Before I could say anything, he whirled around and faced me.

Earlier, I mentioned that the first thing I noticed about him were his eyes, which were bright blue. They sparkled with a sort of aloof amusement peculiar to his character and had considerable intelligence hidden in their azure depths. In addition to his bright eyes, he had flaming red hair that was unruly and hung low over his forehead giving him the impression of dashing youth. His complexion was quite pale, and his skin was very smooth, which completed the look of tender years. But his expression betrayed that he really wasn't much younger than I. He was a little shorter and skinnier than me, and he carried his slender frame with the dignity of a virtuoso and the grace of a dancer.

He sat with an enigmatic smile on his face, studying me for a moment before he spoke in a British accent, enunciating carefully, but speaking quickly and rolling his R's pleasantly.

"Well, my good sir, it seems you have elected to join the living after all. My housekeeper and I were quite worried when you didn't regain consciousness; however, you do appear to have suffered quite a shock."

I was astounded by the fact that he spoke so calmly while I felt as if the world was spinning out of control. I made a valiant effort to contain my emotions and stammered out a sentence as best I could.

"I . . . uh . . . wh-where am I?" I stuttered.

"You are in the sitting room of 37c Montague Street. I tenant these rooms from one Mrs. Montgomery, who has her faults but is an unimpeachable character over all," he replied calmly.

"Montague Street? What city is this?" My bewildered mind seemed to recall having heard that name before somewhere.

"Why, London, of course."

The word London hit me like a ton of bricks, and I collapsed back onto the couch. A horrifying thought occurred to me, and I sat bolt upright. I dreaded the answer, yet asked, "What's the date?"

"August 20, 1892."

The magnitude of my situation struck me. I was in another time and place? How could this be? What happened? Could I get back? If not, then what? I'm in London? In the 19th century? Where would I live? How would I live? Did I even exist in the 21st century anymore? Questions raced through my head. There was a soft knock on the door.

"Ah! Mrs. Montgomery! Please, come in," invited my companion.

I turned and was face-to-face with a kind-looking elderly lady carrying a tea tray. When she saw my face, she seemed perturbed and then looked at my companion disapprovingly. She set the tea tray on the sideboard and walked behind me to turn up the lamp. She then addressed the redhead with a fury that hell hath not.

"Mister Hawkins," she began, "what have you done to this poor fellow? He's as white as a sheet he is!"

"Mrs. Montgomery, I assure you I have 'done' nothing to this man."

"That's the problem then isn't it? That's always the problem." She shook her head admonishingly. "Now then, sir," she said gently as she poured me a cup of tea, "you just sit back and drink this. It'll make you feel better."

She shot the redhead, who was apparently called Mr. Hawkins, another look of derision as she handed him his cup. He smiled genially and thanked her kindly, but with an air of insincerity. She ignored him and turned back to me with a smile. "You'll have to excuse Mister Hawkins. He hasn't any manners," she said in an icy tone. The object of her criticism sipped his tea as though he hadn't heard her.

I attempted to drink the tea, but I preferred coffee, and tea was the last thing I wanted in my agitation.

"So, my good sir, if you feel up to it, I believe it would be appropriate to ascertain your origins so that we–" began Mr. Hawkins, but I cut him off. My nerves couldn't take the strain of them sitting so calmly during such an impossible and inconceivable situation.

"No, you don't understand! First, I was surrounded by trees, then *the eyes* sent me here, and I thought I was dead, but I still had a pulse, so I thought it was a dream, then I screamed at this guy and ran into you, but I don't know what's going on, and I just want to go home or wake up or something! How can you just sit there and be all like 'have some tea, sir' while the world as I know it is gone!" I hadn't meant to be rude to these kind people, but absolute terror is a powerful emotion. Mrs. Montgomery looked incredulous and no doubt thought I had lost my mind, while Hawkins merely looked intrigued.

"He's an American!" She exclaimed in reference to my accent or lack thereof.

"Hush woman, this is neither the time nor the place. Sir, I believe I have been unforgivably rude in my introductions. You see, I am quite unaccustomed to company, and such things do not come naturally to me. My name is Livesey Hawkins, and this, as you may have observed, is Mrs. Montgomery. Now, sir, if I may inquire as to what your name is?"

I sat for a moment in shock, not quite sure what to make of his reaction. I had expected him to call me crazy or a liar, and it almost seemed preferable to have my story denied rather than for him to accept it so easily.

"I can tell when a person is lying; even if I have never met him before. I am an excellent judge of character," said Hawkins nonchalantly.

I stared at him in amazement. He seemed to be reading my thoughts, for I hadn't said anything. He smiled in amusement at my bewildered expression and again inquired as to my name.

"Oh, uh, Andrew, Dr. Andrew, uh, Collins." I replied, still bewildered.

"Well, then, Dr. Collins, it is a pleasure to make your acquaintance. Now then, would you please tell us again, as calmly as possible, just how you came to London?" He pulled a tobacco pipe out of his pocket, but without filling or lighting it, began chewing vigorously on the stem. "Oh, I don't smoke," he said in response to my questioning look, "but you're more than welcome to if you wish."

"No, thank you, I don't smoke either," I replied. I then told him the whole story starting with a few details about my family and ending with waking up in his sitting room. Throughout my narrative, Hawkins sat with his legs criss-cross beneath him on the chair, his fingertips pressed together, and his head inclined so he could stare at me over his hands. When I finished, Mrs. Montgomery, having had remained in the room, looked astounded, but I think she had already made up her mind to believe me when Hawkins proclaimed that I wasn't a liar. He looked up at me with a smile.

"Well, Dr. Collins, it seems that we may have the pleasure of your company for some time. Mrs. Montgomery, would you be good enough to fetch some supper for our guest? He looks quite famished. After all, he has traveled through centuries in order to reach us."

The mystified lady shuffled out of the room, mumbling as she went.

CHAPTER III

A FEW MINUTES AFTER MRS. MONTGOMERY left the room, Hawkins got up from his chair and paced the room in a fit of restless energy, chewing furiously on the stem of his pipe all the while. He seemed to be lost in some deep train of thought, and I was loath to disturb him. He suddenly whirled toward me, his eyes bright, and his pipe poised in his hand.

"Your predicament, Dr. Collins, is indeed very singular," he began.

"I think impossible is more like it," I observed.

"Well, then, surely we are redefining impossible," he said with a smile. "At any rate, I have come to believe that nothing is impossible, my good doctor. At present, I can only see one course of action that is appropriate."

"What's that?" I asked.

"There is an extra room just up the stairs that would suit you nicely, I think, and you are quite welcome to it for as long as you wish. However, you may have to discuss such things with my landlady, as it is her dwelling. We shall also have to see what we can do about getting some proper clothing for you. I may have a set you can borrow for awhile."

"Hold on! That's your course of action—to do nothing?"

"Of course not!" he said as if I had offended him. "I have no intention of doing nothing! There is plenty we can do and to do nothing would be a complete waste."

"If you don't mind me asking," I began tentatively, "why are you helping me?"

"To be completely honest, your story interests me."

"That's not a bad reason." I sat in silence for a moment. "So, there is no way for me to return?"

"There is none that I can see at the moment, but we can start by retracing your steps to the spot where you first arrived and see where that gets us. I will be on my guard in case we discover a way. Ah! Mrs. Montgomery, Dr. Collins is likely to be staying with us for some time, and I think it would be wise to prepare the upstairs bedroom for him if you would be so kind."

Mrs. Montgomery set down on the table the tray she was carrying. "He may stay there for the night, but if he is to be with us awhile, I would prefer to discuss—"

"Yes, yes, fine, whatever." Hawkins cut off and dismissed her with a wave of his hand.

Mrs. Montgomery left the room feeling insulted, almost slamming the door on her way out. I realized that life here was going to be interesting but I hardly realized then just how interesting it would turn out to be. That night, I slept in the spare bedroom upstairs from the sitting room.

I awoke the next day to find that my adventure was not a dream. I was apprehensive about this, but a part of me looked forward to what lay ahead. It was a very odd situation, but I decided that it would be better to accept it as reality until I was proven otherwise. With this attitude in mind, I entered into my new life as a British gentleman.

I went down to the sitting room and found the door ajar. I could hear Hawkins and Mrs. Montgomery speaking.

"Mrs. Montgomery, I am an excellent judge of character," Hawkins contended, "and this fellow has an excellent character. Besides, his story is quite fascinating."

"Fascinating, now there's a word for it," she replied.

"Now then, if he desires, he may stay with us as long as he wishes. If you find that this is acceptable, of course."

"I don't mind having him here, but I can't keep him for free."

"Oh well, you two can work that out. I am perfectly willing to pay his rent, if it comes to that though."

"That's very unusual for you."

"I beg your pardon?"

"It's just that you normally make a habit of avoiding people. If I may ask, why the change of heart?"

"No, you may not ask. Now please leave me alone."

"Very well, but just remember that our visitor is a human being—not a science experiment. You must not merely dismiss him as you do everyone else."

"Be gone!"

I heard her head toward the door. I quickly entered the room as if I had just come down the stairs.

"Good morning, sir," Mrs. Montgomery said with a smile. "I trust you slept well."

"Yeah, um, for the most part. I mean it's a little weird and all you know."

"Yes, I see," she eyed me curiously for a moment, and I wondered what I had said. "I'll fetch your breakfast, sir."

She exited the room, and I was left alone with Hawkins. He was leaning against the mantelpiece with knitted brows, looking into space. He didn't look up at me until I cleared my throat to get his attention.

"Ah, good morning, doctor," he said. "Please, be seated."

I sat down on the sofa, and Hawkins continued to stand at the mantelpiece. "It's a nice place you have here. It seems very, uh, decorative."

"Forgive me, but you have a very interesting manner of speaking. Does everyone in your century talk as you do?" He replied with a curious look.

"Well, yes. I'm actually one of the better ones I think, though."

"How sad."

"What?"

"Oh, it is such a pity that an entire world full of people should have such a vulgar manner of speech. Why do your schools not teach grammar?"

"They do, but—"

"Oh, I see, they are incompetent themselves and cannot hope to achieve anything through their efforts."

"No, the teachers are alright. It's just that—"

"If it is not the teachers, then it must be the pupils. If you are an example of the future for the English language, then I fear that the outlook is very bleak indeed. Oh please, do not be offended my dear fellow, it is merely a fact."

"Don't be offended!" I seldom allow myself to speak out in anger, but Hawkins' whole attitude of superiority was rubbing me wrong, and I wanted to put him in his place. "What am I supposed to be, thrilled? You just insulted me and my entire century—"

"My entire century and me," Hawkins corrected.

"Whatever, you just insulted us, and now you expect me not to react badly to what—"

"Poorly."

"—to what you're saying?"

"'Have said' would most likely work better in that sentence."

"Aw, come on! Look I'm not British, ok?"

"If you were trying to draw my attention to the stack of papers over there, what would you be most likely to say?"

"What does that have to do with anything?"

"Please, humor me."

"Fine. Wait, do you mean these ones here?"

Hawkins snorted disgustedly. "This quite proves my point. You cannot continue to speak as you do, or else people will assume you are mentally unstable."

"I like the way I talk. It works for me," I retorted.

"I find it rather annoying. I will coach you in the proper way to speak, although I am not confident it will accomplish any good."

"But—"

Mrs. Montgomery entered with the breakfast tray just then, and I gave up trying to convince my newfound instructor that I didn't want his help. I concluded that Hawkins seemed a thoroughly unpleasant fellow. He was arrogant, indifferent, and callous. Overall, he was just cold-hearted. However, he had taken me in. There was also something else about him that I couldn't quite understand or even put my finger on. It is like when you think you hear a sound, but you aren't sure whether it was your imagination or not. At any rate, his mannerisms appealed to my psychologist mind, and I was determined to find the reasons for them as well.

After breakfast, Hawkins and I returned to the place where I appeared in London. I was concerned that there would be some difficulty in finding the exact spot, but Hawkins remembered where I had run into him, and I was able to trace my way back to the little dirt lane.

"How very curious!" Hawkins said when we reached the lane. "Are you confident that this is the precise location?"

"Why?"

"I am very familiar with this lane; it has always held some fascination for me. You see, this is where the people whom I called my parents found me."

"Here? You mean this exact spot?"

"Yes."

"I wonder if there is some connection between us."

"I shouldn't be too surprised if there was.

"So, how did they find you?"

"They simply found me." He said impatiently. "Let us walk down the lane and see what we may."

I was still curious about the origins of my new friend, but I was also anxious to find some explanation for my own predicament. Hawkins and I walked down the dirt path, but we could find no clues to get me home or explain how I came to be here in the first place. We gave up. Seeing that I might be in London for some time, Hawkins took me to a tailor's shop and purchased a suit for me. It was odd to be so dressed up, and I have never in my life worn pants with such a high waist. The waistcoat, frock coat, and boots with spats were far different than the clothing I was used to, and I wondered how I was supposed to keep cool since it was summertime. The ensemble was completed by a pair of black leather gloves and a high silk hat. We returned home for noon tea. Then Hawkins left for a couple of hours. Attempting to alleviate my loneliness, I looked for Mrs. Montgomery, hoping to get to know her better. I found her in the kitchen downstairs, chopping vegetables. She was surprised to see me.

"Oh, hello, Mr. Collins, can I help you?" asked Mrs. Montgomery.

"Well, no I guess not. I was just kind of lonely and wanted to see if there was anything I could help you with." She was taken aback and stared at me incredulously, not used to seeing a man in the kitchen, let alone the man who was now a new guest in her house.

"Well, sir, you are a strange one to be sure!"

"So I've been told." I smiled ruefully.

"If you really want to help, I suppose you can start by peeling these potatoes." She handed me a knife, a bucket, and a few large potatoes.

"So, don't you have a maid to help you or something?" I asked as I sat down to my task.

"I did, but she was the laziest creature you ever laid eyes on. I only let her go yesterday."

"Well, what if I helped you out with some of the work around here? Maybe it could cover my board or something."

"It's not respectable work for a man, sir. Surely you would be better off in a different job?"

"Nah, I don't mind. I used to spend my summers cleaning houses so I could earn a little extra money, and I'm used to this sort of stuff."

"That's very kind of you, sir, I would appreciate the help."

From then on, I basically became a sort of male maid. We decided that I would help Mrs. Montgomery for a certain amount of hours each day, and she would in turn consider my board paid.

When Hawkins found out, he made it well known that he disapproved, believing the job women's work, but I continued to help Mrs. Montgomery with her work anyway. She reminded me irresistibly of my grandmother, and her presence comforted me.

Mrs. Montgomery was not a silent person, and I learned a great deal from her. Although she hadn't been too keen about me at first, she quickly warmed up to me, and I soon learned her entire life story. She had started life in the common role of a seamstress but was fortunate to attract the affections of a London banker. They married and purchased 37c Montague Street where they had lived happily for a few years. Her husband, who had always been somewhat sickly, contracted tuberculosis and died. They had no children. She hadn't wanted to sell the house, but she didn't need all of the space, so she decided to lease it to individuals. Hawkins came her way, and he had rented her rooms for many years.

In addition to telling me all about herself, she also taught me some manners. I learned that I should call Livesey Hawkins not by his first name but either Mr. Hawkins or just Hawkins. It was customary to take one's hat off in the presence of a woman. It was inappropriate to smoke in the presence of a lady. I spent hours sitting on a stool in the kitchen peeling potatoes and listening to Mrs. Montgomery talk about the ways of the British. I enjoyed these times.

As I adjusted to what seemed like a primitive way of life, it was the simple things I missed the most—ballpoint pens, flashlights, Kleenexes, hand sanitizer, laundry detergent, and, above all, showers. However, living in a simpler era was refreshing in some ways. I had the opportunity to experience things that other people of my generation had never dreamed of. I was able to see London as it was during Victoria's reign, travel in a horse-drawn cab, and watch as the world progressed during the height of the industrial revolution.

Despite all the fascinating aspects of my adventure, I quickly learned that London wasn't as wonderful as the storybooks make it out to be. The upper class in society lived well in their riches, while the working class slaved away for their meager wages. The poor often didn't survive. The cobblestone streets were congested; diseases, although not as common as they once were, ran rampant; and the air was thick with the smell of coal smoke and sewage.

I noticed that the British spirit was exceptionally buoyant, and most Brits were incredibly patriotic. They adored their Queen, and there were even a few who still wore some token of mourning for the late Prince Albert. They were a truly remarkable people, and, for the most part, I felt I was quite fortunate to be able to live among them.

✳ CHAPTER IV

Without a doubt, the most interesting aspect of London was Livesey Hawkins himself. The man was an absolute puzzle to me, and I vowed to myself that I would figure him out. When I first came to share rooms with him, I noticed he was reclusive and shunned all company except Mrs. Montgomery and me. He was cynical, sarcastic, and subtly rude, but he was also extremely intelligent. These traits combined together made him entertaining when the mood struck him and harsh at other times. He possessed fine manners, but he used them in a mocking and insincere way. He had little patience for simple-minded people, and he would be courteous to them in word and gesture but with dripping sarcasm in his tone of voice. Thus, many people thought him to be odious, although most were too simple-minded to heed his ridicule. He had no friends; indeed, to be called Livesey Hawkins' friend was somewhat of an honor that none had when I arrived in London.

Hawkins was an active man, but in a restless sort of way. He went out for long walks several times a day and avoided talking to anyone as a general rule. I learned that he had been out on one of his strolls when I had run into him. He wasn't very tall, but he set a blazing pace in spite of a slight limp in his left leg due to that leg being a few inches shorter than the other.

Despite his many unpleasant idiosyncrasies, he had a few redeeming qualities. Although he had no regard for his own safety, much to my disapproval, he would not risk the safety of others if he could help it. He also had a great affection for personal hygiene and kept his person very clean and tidy. He liked to be organized, but he hated cleaning even more than he liked organization, so you can imagine the state his belongings were usually in. Mrs. Montgomery and I got into the habit of ganging up on him to keep the sitting room tidy.

For the first few weeks of my stay, my manner of speech greatly annoyed Hawkins. He tolerated me for the most part, but if he was in a bad mood, he wouldn't even let me speak. He made good his threat to coach me in the proper manner of speech, and although I tried very hard I just couldn't learn it. I don't believe this was a result of Hawkins being a poor teacher or me a poor student, but he just wasn't the right teacher for me. He eventually ceased his efforts and wrote me off as a lost cause. One day though, he discovered that although I could not get into the habit of speaking like he wanted, I had picked up a little of it in my writing. After that, my status was elevated from lost cause to a singular individual. In years since, I have improved greatly in both writing and speech, although a little modern lingo slips out from time to time.

I surmised that Hawkins had had a bad childhood, accounting for much of his behavior. However, he rarely spoke about himself and never about his years growing up, so I was left without answers. I then turned to Mrs. Montgomery in order to satisfy my curiosity. The two weren't necessarily close, but they had an understanding: she left him to himself, and he returned the favor. There were many harsh words between them; they were both formidable people, and she wasn't put off by his masterful ways. She tolerated him quite well, despite his inconsideration of her. Although she knew nothing of his childhood, she was able to tell me a bit about his family.

"Mr. Hawkins is a strange one to be sure!" she said to me during one of our conversations. "And even after putting up with him for so long, he still surprises me from time to time—like when he carried you home."

"He carried me home?" I asked with some surprise. "I'm at least three inches taller than him and heavier. How did he manage?"

"Oh, he's quite strong he is. He walked right up to the front door with you slung over his shoulder like a sack of potatoes and said, 'Mrs. Montgomery, please fetch some water, we have a guest,' as if he hadn't done anything more than ask for a cup of tea. I was quite shocked I was."

"Wow! That's pretty weird."

"Yes sir, he seems to find you to be interesting."

I turned back to the table I was scouring with sand—an unpleasant task that made me wish for liquid dish soap—and contemplated my next question. "So, does he have any family?"

"Oh yes, doctor! He has but one family member in this whole world to my knowledge, and that's his sister Agatha. The parents have both passed away."

"Agatha? She sounds pretty. Where is she?"

"She lives on the family estate in the country. Townsend Grange 'tis called. I've never been there, but the house itself sits on about a thousand acres of the best farmland in Surrey. I hear it is quite a lovely place. "

"Wait, doesn't the son inherit land, not the daughter?"

"Well, I don't understand it completely myself. From what I heard, though, Mr. Hawkins didn't want the estate. He asked his father to entail it to Agatha instead, and he receives a portion of the income to live on."

"Hmm. So he has a sister. Is she younger or older?"

"She was born about five years after they found Mr. Hawkins. Her mother died soon after. More than that I don't know."

Because of the large sum he inherited from the estate, Hawkins did not need to work. This put him easily into the upper class of British society, but he preferred a middle-class lifestyle. He also had many talents that he used in his hobbies, although it is hard to say how he occupied himself.

One of his main talents was music, namely, playing the violin. He was very talented and often sat with his eyes closed and played mellifluous melodies that reflected his moods. He could also play well-known pieces when he wished and often treated me to my own private concerts. Music was one of the few things that brought a genuine smile to his sardonic face, and it served as a sturdy ballast during the more turbulent moments in his chaotic life. Many times, I encouraged him to play professionally, but he always smiled that enigmatic smile of his and replied, "That, my dear fellow, would rob me of my chief joy," walking away without another word.

In addition to music, he enjoyed turning his keen intellect to concocting strategies, making it sort of hobby. He advised random people on a course of action when they were presented with an impossible situation, although he wasn't well known and didn't do it often. He also used his skill with strategy on the chessboard when he could find an opponent. When it came to chess, he wasn't merely a master of strategy, he was an artist. He could analyze my thoughts through my body language and actions and then predict almost every move I would make during a chess game. Combining his knowledge of me with that acute intellect of his, he would devise a strategy and beat me in however many moves he wished. He could also do the same thing with a person he had never met before, although the game wasn't so predictable and therefore more challenging and worthwhile. When I realized how good he was, I refused to play chess with him again. To my knowledge, he has only lost one chess game, and—as you will find out—I don't think it really counts. His skill at reading people would've been a psychologist's delight.

Hawkins also reveled in solving riddles and pondering the perplexing problems of life, although he only did this last when there was nothing else to occupy him. You see, his sanity seemed to be preserved through activity, and he would go stir-crazy when there was nothing for him to set his mind upon. For Hawkins, boredom wasn't an option. In fact, I am convinced that his mind was so finely tuned that he would have gone insane without something to brood over.

This was the man I ran into when I first arrived in London, but I noticed a gradual change in him during my stay. At first, he regarded me with the same reserve that he regarded the rest of the world, but by degrees he became less distanced from me I began to see the person he really was. Underneath his callous exterior was a person who was misunderstood and lonely, and I determined to be a friend to him no matter how roughly he might treat me.

My mission of friendship was not received well at first, but I was not to be thwarted. The first sign that I was succeeding came about a month into my London adventure. Hawkins and I were both in the sitting room; he was staring off into space, while I was occupied reading a newspaper. All of a sudden, Hawkins jumped out of his chair and headed for the door, which was a sign that he was going out for one of his restless strolls. He was a man of habit, so I knew that this was the time of day for his second afternoon walk. He would likely be gone for awhile. I was surprised when he paused before going out.

"I say, Collins," he began in his casual manner, "would you care to accompany me for a turn about the neighborhood?"

"You want me to come with you?" I asked, taken aback.

"I would not have asked you if I did not want your company."

"Well, sure! I'll go!" I jumped out of my chair, grabbed my coat and hat and accompanied Hawkins downstairs. Mrs. Montgomery was walking by the stairs when we came down, and I gave her a triumphant smile as we passed. She also smiled and went into another room, humming a song as she went.

We walked in almost complete silence. But after that day, Hawkins started taking me with on his walks. It was as if I had broken through a barrier of some sort. I encouraged him to take an interest in the people around him. Although he tried, he never overcame his cynicism. However, he was genuinely polite to more people.

My mission of friendship was accomplished one morning a few weeks after he began taking me with him on his strolls. I had just finished helping Mrs. Montgomery in the kitchen and went upstairs to join Hawkins in the sitting room. I must've looked exhausted, for as soon as Hawkins saw me, he rang for Mrs. Montgomery.

"You rang, sir?" she asked.

"Yes, Mrs. Montgomery, would you please bring Collins a glass of water? It seems you are a hard taskmistress, and my friend looks quite parched." She and I both jumped when he said the word friend, but we were smart enough not to say anything about it. I had broken through Hawkins' last barrier. After that, I had his complete confidence.

I had thought I had fixed Hawkins and, therefore, saved him from a lonely life. I realize now that he fixed me too. I had never had a real friend in my life, and I wasn't accustomed to earning a friendship. In fact, I didn't even know what friendship really meant until I tried to teach it. I was shocked to learn that it goes deeper than I originally thought. I had always strived to be surrounded by as many people as possible, but the friendship that I earned with Hawkins was more rewarding than any popularity I had ever had.

✳ CHAPTER V

SUMMER FADED INTO AUTUMN WITH THE usual fanfare of nature. The thick London fog smoothly eddied in every chance it had. The weather was mostly wet, but since I was originally from western Washington, I wasn't bothered much. Hawkins' characteristic limp tended to worsen in wet weather, but he ignored it and walked with a quick stride nonetheless. Mrs. Montgomery, on the other hand, needed my help even more on rainy days since the cold weather did nothing to ease her aches.

Every Saturday was washing day at 37c Montague Street, and it was Saturday that I dreaded the most. What we of the modern world accomplished through a washer and dryer, Mrs. Montgomery did by hand, and I admired her greatly for her strength. The first time I helped her, I was sore for days from wringing out the soaked cloth.

"Come on now, doctor, if I can do it you can too," she said to me as we did laundry on the first Saturday of October. I looked down at my blistered hands and then at the large stack of clothing and linens with a sigh.

"I think the laundry is breeding, Mrs. M," I groaned. "Wasn't the pile that big an hour ago?"

She laughed and continued scrubbing a shirt against the

ridged washboard. "We've made some progress, I'm sure. The pile isn't as large as you imagine, and we'll be done with it before long." She caught my dubious look and smiled. "As soon as you're finished here you can go, doctor. I won't need you for the rest of the day."

"Sweet!" I returned to my work with renewed vigor.

She was right, of course, and I rejoiced when all of the laundry was strung across the scullery to dry. I went up to the sitting room, only to find it deserted. Hawkins had apparently gone out for his walk, and I was crestfallen that he hadn't waited for me. Our walks together were the highlight of my day, and I looked forward to them because they provided a means for me to observe my odd friend somewhat closely. It actually surprised me that he had gone out without me, for he would usually say something if he wanted to be alone. I heard a slight noise behind me, and I whirled around to see Hawkins coming out of his bedroom with his gloves and hat in his hand. He looked up at me and smiled genially.

"Good day to you doctor, shall we head out?"

"Oh, uh, yeah! Let's go."

Our walk was wet at the outset, but by the time we headed back the sun was shining brightly. We didn't take a long walk, partially due to the cold and because I was exhausted from washing day. We made it back to the house before the clock struck two.

The rest of the afternoon promised to be uneventful, and I decided to spend it reading the newspaper. Hawkins took up his pipe and a thick book, sprawled himself out upon the couch, and started reading. Hawkins didn't often read, but every once in awhile the mood would strike. When it did, heaven help whoever tried to disturb him. After a few minutes into our restful afternoon, there was a soft knock at the door. Mrs. Montgomery entered.

"Mr. Hawkins?" she asked cheerfully.

"For God's sake what is it?" was the gruff reply.

"A letter for you sir," Mrs. Montgomery replied with some asperity.

"Who from?"

"Your sister."

Hawkins sighed impatiently. "Oh, bother the dear girl anyway. Put it on the table. I shall read it later."

She set the letter on the table and left the room, shooting an exasperated look at me on her way out the door. I smiled sympathetically over the top of my paper and continued perusing it while the room once again fell silent except for the bold ticking of the clock on the mantelpiece.

After a few moments, Hawkins' curiosity got the better of him. With a growl, he slammed his book shut and jumped up from the couch. He grabbed the letter off the table and tore it open somewhat violently. Once he had read the contents, he sighed wearily and dropped into a chair.

"My sister," he began, "begs me to come visit her."

"That's not so bad. It kind of sounds fun." I was eager to meet his sister, and a trip to the countryside sounded marvelous after my few months in the city. I knew it would've been rude to ask if I could accompany him. I hoped he might invite me.

He studied me with a peculiar expression for a moment, and a mischievous light sprang into his eyes. "Oh yes, I suppose it would be somewhat of a treat." He said as he leaned back in his chair with his hands behind his head. "Townsend Hall is lovely year-round, but autumn is quite exceptional in my opinion. My sister, Miss Agatha Hawkins, is a very gracious host, and her cook makes the best beef brisket I have ever tasted, not to mention the homemade blackberry jam. Of course, you would want to stay here with Mrs. Montgomery while I am away so you would not be inconvenienced." He looked at me askance. I felt deflated—not yet having learned to recognize his perverse sense of humor.

"Oh," was all I could manage to say.

He smiled for a moment and feigned indifference. "Of course," as he made a thorough inspection of his pipe, "if you want to come along, I'm sure something could be arranged."

My spirits instantly rose, and I sat up in my chair in excitement. "I would love to go!" I exclaimed.

"Splendid!" He said as he jumped to his feet. He walked over to the desk and scribbled something on a slip of paper. "We will leave tomorrow at noon. In the morning, we will get whatever you will need for our stay. It shall be our holiday, our escape from the wearisome jungle that is London. You will find yourself better for the fresh air also, I imagine."

"Shouldn't we let your sister know we are coming?"

"That is what I am doing, my dear fellow!" He brandished the piece of paper with a flourish, and I was astounded by how quickly he could go from prostration to bustling energy. For a moment, I wondered if he might be bipolar. He threw open the door with a grand gesture, and trotted down the staircase while shouting for Mrs. Montgomery. His good moods were almost as frightening as his bad ones.

The next morning, we shopped for travel items for me. I had little time to pack. Full of energy, Hawkins was in a rush to leave and admonished me to move swiftly. Hawkins hummed to himself cheerfully and harassed Mrs. Montgomery. However, we were finally ensconced in a cab with our luggage on our way to Waterloo Station, and our good landlady waved goodbye from the bottom doorstep.

I'VE NEVER HAD A PARTICULAR liking for trains, but when I saw the old-fashioned steam engine waiting for us, I was excited. She was a beauty of an engine in the true British style, but I knew the ride would be somewhat less comfortable than the trains of my native century. Hawkins had reserved an entire first-class compartment for the two of us. It wasn't long before we were going down the rails toward Surrey.

The entire train ride, I stared out the window at the scenery as city gave way to green country. The rolling green hills were dotted with farm buildings that stood boldly in their solitude with stone walls cutting across the pastures. I spotted both sheep and cattle in some of the fields, in addition to the plant life common to England.

I have always been excited about car rides, and this train ride reminded me of driving down Yelm Highway from Lacey to Yelm. The scenery of modern Yelm Highway was vastly different than the countryside of England, but it still reminded me of Washington.

While I was busy in my surveillance of the scenery, Hawkins slept soundly on the bench opposite me. He was normally a light sleeper—when he slept—but I suppose there was something about the train ride that acted as a sedative. He always seemed drowsy when we rode in a cab. It was just another one of his many idiosyncrasies.

When we finally arrived in Farnham Station, there was a nice four-wheeled carriage waiting for us, compliments of the Lady of Townsend Hall. The driver was an amiable fellow. He seemed very glad to see Hawkins, although he didn't actually say anything to that affect. In fact, the chap didn't say anything at all but only smiled at us genially.

The carriage trip took us through Farnham and then onto a lonely road, where we passed few pedestrians along the way. It was actually sunny out that day as we drove through the countryside, but the clouds were threatening to block out the light and warmth. I was still extremely excited and it was difficult to sit still. Hawkins lounged comfortably with an amused smile on his face. Our driver must have hated me by the time the trip was over because I nearly talked his ear off. Although I tried, I couldn't get a word out of him. Hawkins finally informed me that the driver was a mute. I was embarrassed to say the least. I turned my barrage of questions at Hawkins. "So, tell me" I said to him, "what's Townsend Hall like?"

"It is a beautiful place, but I fear that words can hardly do it justice."

"Oh."

"Indeed. The date the hall was built is unknown due to the fact that all papers on the subject have been destroyed. However, it is conjectured that an edifice of some sort was in place as early as 1652. The current hall, however, is surrounded by 2,000 acres of fertile farmland, much of which is tenanted to farmers. My sister manages the estate with the help of Mr. Joseph Westfield, her overseer. A domestic staff keeps the hall in order, there is a staff for the stables and estate, and gardeners maintain the grounds."

Hawkins continued, "A few decades ago, the back quarters of Townsend Hall were consumed in a fire, and my great grandfather, who managed the estate at the time, did not have the money to have them rebuilt. He left the back quarters off and had the remaining part of the house re-walled. When Agatha took over after the death of our father, she installed gas lines and indoor plumbing. The house had fallen into disrepair, but she's done much to restore it—even beyond its previous greatness."

"Sounds cool. Anything else I should know?"

"A creek runs through part of the property. Agatha calls it Aula Creek. It is lovely this time of year. Are you quite satisfied?"

"No, but I'll wait until we get there to ask more questions."

We fell into silence, and I studied the land around me as we bounced along. We were on a lonely stretch of road that ran through a wooded area, and the sun shone fitfully between the branches overhead. I had noticed a few dwellings when we exited Farnham, especially one large estate. Townsend Hall was a full six miles away from the village.

We neared a bend in the road when Hawkins sat up in his seat and pointed through the trees in front and a little to the left of us. "That, my dear loquacious fellow, is Townsend Hall."

✳ CHAPTER VI

THE HALL OF TOWNSEND GRANGE WAS A radiant example of British architecture. The house was very large with multiple gables and a vine-enshrouded front. It was constructed with timber and red brick with a tiled roof atop its two stories. I was captured by it from the start. I could also see some of the outbuildings, which were constructed in a similar fashion to the hall. There were perfect green lawns on either side of the long driveway. I felt as though I was driving up to a castle through a fairy tale land in order to meet the fairy queen herself. The best was yet to come.

Agatha Hawkins stood on the front porch with a wide smile on her face. I was sure that I had never seen anything so lovely in all my life. Agatha did not particularly resemble her brother, which wasn't surprising since they weren't siblings by blood. Where he had red hair, hers was a lovely chocolate brown. She had beautiful green eyes instead of his bright blue ones. She stood straight and prim as any good woman in the era should. Strength was written into the curve of her shoulders, but with an air of disarming girlishness. She was a little taller than her brother but shared the gracefulness and dignity common to them both. As we climbed out of the carriage, she laughed and quickly ran toward her brother.

"My dear brother it is wonderful to see you again!" she said, embracing him warmly.

"Aggie! How are you on this fine day, dear girl?" Hawkins answered.

"I am quite well, thank you." She paused to straighten his jacket and smiled. "Well, you're looking a sight more cheerful than last I saw you. I do worry about you, you know."

"And quite needlessly, I assure you." He turned toward me with a grand sweep of his arm. "Aggie, this is my dear friend, Dr. Andrew Collins."

She looked at me, and I was completely transfixed. "It is very nice to meet you, Dr. Collins, but if you stand there like that much longer, I fear you may capture flies." She giggled, and offered me her hand.

I realized that I had been staring at her with my mouth open and roused myself with a start, quickly pulling my hat off and blushing in embarrassment. She still had her hand out to me, and I embraced it in my own shaking fingers.

"Aggie!" Hawkins said in a mock scold. "Mind your manners, dear girl."

"I am so terribly sorry, sir; I do beg your pardon." She smiled, curtseying gracefully. I played with my hat bashfully.

"Why don't we give a tour for the good doctor, Aggie?" suggested Hawkins. "He is quite new to England, and he has never seen a good British hall before."

"What an excellent idea! Come this way, gentlemen."

Agatha smiled at me radiantly and started to walk away. Hawkins leaned over to me and whispered, "Offer her your arm," holding his arm out to demonstrate. I caught up to Agatha and offered her my arm with as much gallantry as I could muster. She smiled, linked her arm through mine, and led the way toward the house. Hawkins followed with his hands behind his back, beaming broadly.

Townsend Hall was like a geode. While the outside was somewhat plain, the inside was sparkling and gorgeous. We were admitted by Agatha's butler, who only had one arm, into the grandiose house. The tile floor was well-polished, the walls were hung with grand paintings, and the whole ambience of the old building spoke of the grand people who had entered through these doors. Hawkins and I hung our coats on an elegant coat rack, and Agatha gave orders to her butler that our luggage should be brought in. We then took a tour of Townsend hall.

There were more rooms than I could remember in the main wing of the house; among them was a ballroom, a capacious dining room, a parlor or sitting room, a morning room, a billiard room, library, an office of some sort, and a drawing room. It would take too much time to describe each room in detail, and even then I would not have done them justice. They were all luxurious rooms and each seemed to have a personality of its own. The bedrooms were located upstairs, and the west wing belonged to the servants. The east wing held the nursery, school room, and other children's rooms, although there were no children in the house at that time. The scullery, kitchen, cellar, and other work rooms were below the ground floor.

Throughout the tour, my arm remained linked in Agatha's, and I took in the grandeur of the house while thrilled by her presence. She and Hawkins talked back and forth, telling me about the various curiosities in the house, and I asked a question every now and then. It was all fascinating, yet the house had a sad history as far as the Hawkins' family was concerned. Many members of the family had met their end within these walls, but their memories would live on as long as the house stood.

It was past noon when we finished our tour. Agatha proposed we have lunch. I learned that due to Hawkins' excellent sense of timing—it was excellent in that he knew just when it would be the most inconvenient—we arrived on the day that Agatha had been invited to attend a ball at the home of a neighboring squire. I believed that Hawkins had hoped that we might have the entire house to ourselves that evening, but Agatha was used to her odd brother, and she was prepared. She had secured invitations for us for the evening and I was excited. But Hawkins sulked as he sipped his tea.

After lunch, it started to rain, which meant a tour of the grounds was out of the question. We took refuge in the parlor.

"Dr. Collins," Agatha asked me, "do you play any musical instruments?"

"No, I don't. I wish I had learned as a kid, but I never really got around to it." By this time, I had overcome my initial nervousness and discovered that I was comfortable around Agatha.

"Ah, well we may have to teach you then, won't we brother?" she replied.

"I think you might find better success than I. It seems I am a poor teacher." Hawkins retorted.

"A poor teacher? What on earth were you trying to teach him?"

"He was trying to teach me how to talk," I answered.

Agatha looked at me with astonishment. "It would seem as though you speak fairly well. I do admit that there is something odd about your choice of words, but I do not see why you should need lessons."

Hawkins then explained my actual origins to Agatha. Throughout his narrative, she looked alarmed but intrigued. "How interesting!" she exclaimed. "You have traveled through time and yet I would have been prepared to swear that you had been born in the 1800s. You have done very well, Dr. Collins. How are you enjoying our century?"

I sighed in relief, glad to be accepted by this lovely young lady. "I love it. There are a few things I've had a hard time with, but for the most part it's been nice."

"Oh, I am glad to hear it! You are quite welcome at Townsend Grange whenever you wish."

"Thanks!" Our eyes met, and I realized that I was in love.

AROUND TWO O'CLOCK in the afternoon, I felt drowsy as I climbed the stairs next to Hawkins. It had been a sensational day. Hawkins had noticed my fatigue and suggested tha t I rest before the evening ahead, since it was unlikely that I would get any sleep that night. A nap sounded great. Apparently the ball wouldn't start until late and would last well into the morning. The one-armed butler led the way upstairs to our rooms, which were located right next to each other on the second floor.

"Sleep well, old chap," said Hawkins as he entered his room.

"Yeah, you, too," I replied groggily. I went in my room, collapsed into the four-poster bed, and promptly fell asleep.

A maid woke me up a few hours later. "Her ladyship wants to leave in about an hour." She left me with a light meal of biscuits and a glass of milk.

I was enthusiastic for the ball and even more so to see Agatha again. I prepared as best I could. My British suit was a formidable creature; I had to ask Hawkins for his assistance. He was in a bad mood and not looking forward to that evening's festivities. He sat on my bed after he helped me, chewing furiously on his pipe and sulking.

"Aw come on, Hawkins," I said in an endeavor to cheer him up, "it isn't as bad as all that. Dances are a lot of fun. Or at least that's what I hear. I always made sure I was busy when a high school dance came around."

"Fun indeed!" he snorted with contempt, "people dressed up in their finest all for the sake of besting each other. It's about as enjoyable as cholera."

"You're being cynical again," I said as I struggled with my bow tie. "Social gatherings give you an opportunity to meet new people—"

"Humph!" he scoffed derisively.

"What's so bad about that?" I asked in exasperation.

"Everything."

"That's not an answer."

"It is my answer, and the only one you shall get."

"You're such a pain sometimes."

He sat silently for a moment, chewing thoughtfully. "Allow me to ask you a question. What do you find so pleasing about meeting new people?"

I thought for a moment before replying. "Well, I suppose I get some satisfaction over being sociable, for one. There's also the opportunity to make new friends."

"You could just as easily make new enemies. Why take the risk?"

"It's worth the risk if you make a new friend. Besides, most people are at least polite to you when you meet them, so there's really no harm done most of the time."

"Ah, but what's the purpose of it all?"

"Why do I get the feeling you're leading me somewhere with this conversation?"

His eyes twinkled mischievously. "Please, just answer the question."

"It looks like it all comes back to being social."

"Exactly! So, by being social, one is actually satisfying one's desire to be accepted. Do you agree?"

"Yeah, that makes sense."

"And you will, of course, also agree that most if not all people who attend social gatherings are striving to fit in?"

"That seems pretty obvious."

"Thus, you have obtained the answer to your initial inquiry."

"Wait, you're saying that dances are bad because people want to fit in? That's stupid!"

"You wanted an answer."

"And now you're getting a question. What the heck is wrong with trying to fit in?"

"It is simple. Why follow the masses when you can be your own being?"

"Yeah and die alone? No thanks, I'd rather take the dark path of trying to be accepted." I was still struggling to tie my bow tie and started my third attempt.

"But it is so freeing to not care about being accepted. You really must try it some time."

"You know what your problem is? You're afraid of people. You're scared to death of what they will say about you, so you pretend that you don't care and then give them reason to despise you. It's pretty obvious that you're protecting yourself. Look, I'm a psychologist. Social psychology is my specialty, and I know that people need other people. You really have to get out more."

He sat silently for a moment, taken aback—or so I thought—and then continued on as before.

"No, I believe you are quite mistaken. I am not afraid of people, and I certainly do not need protecting."

"Denial."

"No."

"This is pointless. Someday you're going to be completely alone, and then you will realize that it's not so great. I promise I won't say 'I told you so' when it happens."

"I am—rest assured—that such a moment would not affect me as deeply as you believe. In time, you will agree with me, I am sure.

Ha! I got it!" I exclaimed joyously as I admired my newly tied bow tie. Hawkins eyed me critically and laughed.

"My dear Collins, I am afraid you have tied it upside down. Let me assist you so that we may be off."

Hawkins set my tie straight quickly with his practiced hand. We left my room and went downstairs, clothed as only English gentlemen can be. I felt like I was straight out of Phantom of the Opera. Wearing a black cape, top hat, and white gloves and sporting a cane only served to heighten this impression. Hawkins was dressed similarly to me and, with his usual stately manner, bore his attire very well. Agatha met us at the bottom of the stairs. She looked radiant in a red gown.

"Gentlemen, you both look very handsome this evening," she said, "but my dear brother, you have not even troubled to comb your hair."

"And I have no intention of doing otherwise," said Hawkins.

Agatha sighed resignedly, and gave me a look of mock helplessness. "Ah well, I suppose it can't be helped. Come, we must be on our way."

❄ CHAPTER VII

THE BALLROOM WAS FILLED WITH WOMEN in twirling skirts who gracefully floated across the floor with their smartly dressed partners. The dance was a lively and complex one. I was among the men who stood along the wall, staring longingly into the mass of gaiety. Hawkins stood beside me, sipping a glass of punch and looking as bored as he possibly could while trying to remain hidden. You see, there was one young lady who had made the mistake of being attracted to my stoic friend, and she was pining to get a dance with him. She was young and one of those silly type of girls who giggle nonstop. Since her father happened to be the host of the event, she was trying to convince him to ask Hawkins to dance with her. She seemed to be quite popular among the gentlemen, but she had made herself a wallflower in order to carry out her plot. For her sake, I hoped that her infatuation would wear off quickly, but she wasn't the only young lady in the room smitten by my friend's good looks. She was the only one daring—or stupid—enough to try to dance with him, though.

Agatha was not with us for very long before Lord Prescott Trelawney Roberts—with an air of extreme pride—asked her to dance. He looked at her like a prize to be won and occasionally cast a haughty glance at the other men in the room. He clearly felt superior to us all, especially me since I didn't know how to dance. I hated to watch.

"What a jerk," I said to Hawkins in reference to Lord Roberts.

"A jerk. I am learning your language Collins, but I'm not familiar with that term. It sounds rather harsh for you."

"It means he's a very unlikable guy."

"Ah, you mean Lord Roberts. He and I have a mutual understanding."

"You do?"

"Yes, he loathes me, and I despise him."

I laughed. "Well, at least you can outdo him in some areas. I can't even dance."

Hawkins sipped his punch some more and waved his fingers lightly to the music. "A sprightly tune, don't you agree?"

"Sure." I stared sullenly out into the ballroom where I could see Agatha dancing with that odious man.

"You are captured by my sister, are you not?" Hawkins asked quietly. I jumped at the suddenness of the question and blushed.

"Well, I, uh, she is very pretty." I stammered. He was about to reply when our host approached us.

"Good evening, Mr. Hawkins and Dr. Collins," he said amiably. He twirled the ends of his gray mustache in his fingers. "I hope you gentlemen are enjoying yourselves."

"Indeed we are, Mr. Higgins. It is a lively party," Hawkins replied.

"I cannot help but feel it would be livelier if we could prevent the acquisition of wallflowers."

"I haven't noticed a peculiarly large amount this evening," Hawkins replied.

"I see one over there," he gestured to his lovely blonde daughter, who was standing against a wall. "See how she stares forlornly into the ballroom? It is a pity that she has no one to dance with, and doubly so since they are soon to start the quadrille, her favorite dance. You will also observe that she is my daughter."

"She is a lovely young lady, and I have little doubt that a

gentleman will ask her to dance."

"All the gentlemen already have partners. I hate to impose upon the two of you, but would one of you honor my daughter, Miss Francis, with a dance? I would be a very grateful host."

I saw the color drain from Hawkins' face. He turned pleadingly toward me. I held up my hands and shook my head. "Sorry, I can't dance."

"But—" Hawkins started to say.

Mr. Higgins continued, "Oh, Mr. Hawkins, it would honor me greatly if you danced with my daughter. Your sister, Miss Agatha, tells me that you are a very fine dancer."

Hawkins looked at our host's imploring face and sighed resignedly. "Fine."

"Very good sir! I am sure she will be pleased," Higgins said.

Hawkins scowled at me as I struggled to contain my laughter and then pasted on his most captivating smile as he made his way toward the young Miss Francis Higgins.

"Ha! Boy, this should be interesting," I said to my host. He nodded his head in agreement.

"Yes, I admit that I am adverse to the idea, but my daughter was insistent, and she allied herself to my wife."

I nodded my understanding.

"I have known Mr. Hawkins since he was young, and I am quite convinced that my daughter is a poor match for him. She is far too simple and he too complex. Hopefully this will prove to douse her desire, and then she might see reason at last. Good evening to you, sir." He moved off through the ballroom, greeting guests, and being a good host.

I turned my attention back toward Hawkins who by this time had made his way to his prospective dance partner. The music for the current song had ceased, and partners for the next dance were lining up. The young lady started slightly when Hawkins approached her. Hawkins bowed gracefully while Miss Francis appeared barely able to contain her excitement as she curtseyed. He gave me a look that betrayed his extreme distaste, readjusted his charming smile, and then gallantly led her by the hand into the middle of the ballroom. She strutted by his side, seemingly determined to show the whole party who she was dancing with. I was sympathetic to my friend, but I had hopes that dancing would be good for him. Just then, Agatha appeared at my side, out of breath from her last dance.

"Agatha! Oh, I mean Miss Hawkins."

"Good evening, Dr. Collins, I hope you are enjoying yourself," she said breathlessly. I pulled up a chair for her, and she sat down gratefully.

"Yes, actually I am."

"My goodness, is that Livesey out there with Miss Francis?" she asked incredulously.

"Yeah, she convinced Mr. Higgins to ask Hawkins to dance with her. It looks like she has a crush on him or something."

Agatha giggled, and I grinned. The music for the quadrille started, and the lively dance began. Hawkins danced with his usual grace, but I noticed that his dance partner seemed to be flaunting herself more than anything. It was like watching a bird try to attract the attention of a stone statue, but she was not to be daunted. They talked all the while they executed the intricate steps of the dance, when she suddenly stopped and slapped Hawkins across the face. The dance came to halt, and the room went dead silent. Miss Francis Higgins turned from her former idol and ran from the room crying with her distraught mother at her heels. Hawkins stood for a moment, stunned, and joined Agatha and I along the wall. The dance resumed.

"What happened?" I asked.

He rubbed the red spot on his cheek where her hand had collided with his face. "I am not certain on that point. Ladies are such fickle beings at times. I merely inquired if she preferred to ride a horse a straddle or sidesaddle."

Mr. Higgins approached us, looking appalled. "Mr. Hawkins, I must extend my deepest apologies for this embarrassing episode. I assure you the girl will be dealt with, and you have my word that such a thing will never happen again."

"It is quite alright, my dear sir. There is no harm done. I do advise that in the future you be a little wary of your daughter's dance partners."

He nodded and caught his wife's scowl from across the room. "Please excuse me gentlemen, Miss Agatha." He strode across the room to be scolded by his formidable wife.

The three of us stood in silence, watching the rest of the dance, which got on fairly well in spite of its odd interruption. When it was coming to a close, I noticed that Lord Roberts headed our way.

"Hawkins," I whispered, "the jerk is returning."

He followed my gaze calmly. "Indeed. What of it?"

"Isn't there something we can do?"

"Asking Agatha to dance comes to mind."

"I can't dance!"

"Collins, I believe the next dance is a slow waltz. Just take Agatha to a corner of the ballroom where you won't be in the way, and I'm sure you'll be fine."

"You really think so?"

"You had better ask her now, he is almost upon us."

I turned to Agatha. "Uh, Miss Hawkins, do you, uh—" My mind went blank, and I couldn't remember the proper way to ask.

"I believe you are about to ask me for the honor of a dance," she said with a smile.

"Oh, yeah, actually I was."

"It would be my pleasure." She picked up the edge of her skirt, and I took her hand. Lord Roberts had just come around to the other side of Hawkins, and I looked back to flash him a look of triumph. Roberts returned my look with indignant anger.

The quadrille had just ended. Agatha and I found a spot where we wouldn't be in the way of the other dancers. I warned her that I didn't know what I was doing, but she only smiled and said she would instruct me. The music started, and I took a deep breath before taking Agatha's hand. I glanced at Hawkins, and he smiled radiantly. There was no sign of Lord Roberts.

I must've been the worst dancer on the floor that night, but

Agatha and I were by far having the most fun. She encouraged me when I failed, and we laughed as I tried my best to imitate those around me while avoiding Agatha's feet. I saw the smile disappear from Agatha's face, as I felt someone tap me on the shoulder. I turned around and was face-to-face with Lord Roberts.

"Excuse me, my good sir," he said bitingly. "But you are dancing with my partner. It would be to your advantage to withdraw immediately."

I would be lying if I said I wasn't intimidated by this man. I was tall and stout. He stood taller and boasted more muscle. However, I decided that I wasn't going to just leave Agatha like some coward. I swallowed my fear and stood up to him.

"No, actually Miss Hawkins is my partner right now. You had your turn, and I suggest you leave us in peace."

Roberts recoiled as though I had flung mud on his white waistcoat.

"How dare you speak to me in such a fashion, you insolent fool! This is outrageous! I have never been treated with such impertinence in my entire life!"

I felt my courage building and replied, "Well, then maybe it's about time." I suddenly found myself lying on the floor with a fist-shaped bruise forming on my face. Agatha was kneeling over me. I saw Roberts coming at me to finish what he had started. The music had ceased once more, and all the couples gawked at us. I had the feeling that I was about to get the stuffing beat out of me, when all of a sudden Hawkins casually stepped between me and Roberts.

"Excuse me, Lord Roberts, I cannot help but observe that your actions have been unforgivably rude."

"If you do not remove yourself this instant, Mr. Hawkins, I will be forced to remove you."

"It would give me great pleasure to see you try." Roberts, who no doubt weighed at least a hundred pounds more than Hawkins, came at the brave redhead, but he was no match for my friend's agility. The fight lasted only a few seconds and ended with Roberts lying dazed on the floor, while Hawkins inspected his damaged knuckles.

"Have you had enough, or do you wish for more?" inquired Hawkins.

Roberts was about to say something but changed his mind, got up, and left the room in a fit of rage. He stopped at the door, obviously determined to have the last word. "Hawkins, you have not seen the last of me!"

"Lord Roberts, if you have not had enough this evening, I am quite able to repeat my performance at any time and any place. However, if you wish to avoid mutilating your handsome features, I would advise that you avoid threatening me. I am a dangerous man to have as an enemy." Hawkins' eyes blazed, and Roberts could not hold his stare. He turned and left the room, nursing his bleeding nose.

"Now then, Collins, are you alright?" He asked as he pulled me to my feet.

"Yeah, I think so. He only hit me once, right?"

"Yes, my dear fellow. Agatha, I think it would be best if we cut our evening short and leave now." She nodded silently.

Hawkins turned to address the room. "My dear people, I am terribly sorry for this incident. Please, enjoy the rest of your evening."

Agatha and Hawkins escorted me out of the building, pausing to apologize to the host, and then headed home.

THE NEXT FEW DAYS at Townsend Grange were wonderful. The late autumn weather with its accompanying rain couldn't hide the fabulous scenery. Before the week was out, I officially declared that Agatha and I were courting. To my surprise, Hawkins approved and encouraged our relationship however he could. Sometimes when the three of us were together, he made excuses to leave our company so Agatha and I could be alone. Other times, he might suggest that she show me some obscure plant that grew on the grounds. And once, he even opted to dine in the kitchen with the cook so that we might have a romantic meal. Neither Agatha nor I protested too much, and he had a knack for not overdoing it so that we would have just enough time to ourselves as is healthy for the beginning of a relationship.

It was clear that Hawkins adored his sister, and I was fascinated observing the change that came over him when he was in her presence. His eyes sparkled with warmth that was almost human, and his pale face radiated with a genuine smile. He was also very protective of her, which she found to somewhat irritating. He would leap off a cliff if it would keep her from harm. Agatha adored her brother also, and she tended to look up to him in most respects. She also worried about him and was glad that I had become his friend.

Agatha possessed her brother's talent for music, save that she preferred the piano. Hawkins had brought his violin from London, and he and Agatha played duets that were as entertaining to watch as to listen to. They communicated back and forth with their eyes throughout the performance, challenging each other until they came to a dramatic finale, leaving them too exhausted to play anymore. They played together most evenings, either making up their own duets or playing pieces well known to me. Agatha started to teach me to play the piano, and she was a patient teacher despite my inability to grasp the complexities of the instrument. When they didn't entertain me with their musical prowess, they engaged in a game of chess. They had been playing this same game for nearly a decade without a winner because they were both that good. However, since the chess game tended to consume their entire attention, for my sake they didn't play often.

Other days, I took walks through the large garden with its latent beauty, perused the large collection of leather-bound books, or just enjoyed myself however I wished. The three of us took several rides through the countryside; other days we stayed at the hall and lounged as the rain fell and danced with the wind. It is pleasant to be completely free of obligations, but all vacations must come to an end.

November 29 was to be our last day at Townsend Grange. Agatha was leaving the next day to visit a friend in Paris. We had the option of staying at the hall for as long as we wished, but

Hawkins needed to return to London, and I didn't want to stay by myself. Our last day quickly overtook us, going by far too fast. Agatha and I had both been preoccupied during the day, and we hardly saw each other until after supper was over. We stole a few moments alone together, for it would be our last for quite some time.

We walked in silence through the dormant garden and watched the sun sink from the clear sky. Neither of us seemed willing to say anything—words would have ruined the moment anyway. We came to a stone bench beneath a cherry tree and sat down for some time as day gradually turned to night.

"Hey, Aggie, can you tell me about your family?" I asked. We were silent for some time. It seemed that Aggie was hesitant about sharing.

"My family? What would you like to know?"

"Well, what was your dad like?"

"My father was a great man, a terrible man, and a broken man." She said softly. "My father loved my mother deeply. When she died giving me life, it broke him. He despised me as much as he had loved her. I believe I would not have survived if it had not been for Livesey. He protected me from my father and earned his scorn as well. My father took to isolation, and eventually we would not see him for days."

"What happened after that?"

"Oh, my father began to climb out of his isolation after awhile, and he repented of his actions. He tried to be a father to us, but Livesey wanted nothing to do with him. Livesey went away to boarding school, and I was dreadfully afraid that something terrible would happen. However, once I understood that my father was merely a sad and lonely man, I pitied him and grew to love him. We were on good terms when he died, although Livesey never quite made up with him."

"Gee. That's rough."

"It could have been far worse."

"You know, Livesey is a really weird name."

"It is actually a nickname that I gave him long ago. You are familiar with Robert Louis Stevenson's *Treasure Island?*"

"Yeah, I've read it."

"It was published when I was young. Although it was more of a boy's book, my brother read it to me. The character, Dr. Livesey, reminded me of him, and I gave him that nickname."

"What's his real name?"

"William Scott Jeremiah Hawkins."

"Holy cow! That's quite a name!"

"William Scott is in honor of our father. Most people know him as Jeremy."

"Ah. So what's your name?"

"Agatha Cecilia Primrose Hawkins."

"I like that name. It is as pretty as you are."

She smiled. We sat in silence, watching the moon rise through the bare branches of the cherry tree.

It was dark when we decided to return to the hall. A full moon watched us from high in the clear sky. I could see my breath in the night air, but I didn't feel cold at all. We sauntered through the shrubbery, which was just a little eerie, and saw the lights of the grand old house. Just outside the French windows that led from the garden into the parlor, Agatha stopped me, and we shared a kiss in the moonlight.

The thing they say about a first kiss making your knees weak is absolutely true, by the way, and I had to sit down for a moment after she went inside. Although I was nearly thirty, I had never kissed anyone before, and the feeling burned pleasantly in my mind. I will never forget my visit to the English countryside where I found my true love or the kiss we shared under the moonlight. I retired to my room in absolute bliss that night and had pleasant dreams of moonlit gardens until the rooster heralded a new day.

❋ CHAPTER VIII

THE TRIP BACK TO LONDON WASN'T nearly as wonderful as the trip out to the countryside. Hawkins once again slept the train ride away, and I stared dolefully out the window thinking about Agatha and missing her as the rain drops raced each other down the glass. The green countryside eventually gave way to the drab splendor of the city, and we were once more in London.

After the long ride, we were ready to stretch our legs. Hawkins ordered our luggage sent home, and we started to walk. After some time, my eye fell on a comfortable-looking pub. Neither Hawkins nor I were drinking men, but I felt a stiff drink would do both of us good. It took some convincing to get Hawkins inside, and even then he wasn't too thrilled, but I was sure it would be worth it.

The pub was warm and dry, dim and hazy. The few people in there were busy smoking, drinking, and talking. Some glanced at us when we walked in. We approached the polished bar where the landlord stood cheerily and ordered a couple of beers—or ale as they say. Standing at the bar sipping our drinks, a huge gentleman walked by us. He was round, muscular, and at least six feet tall. His presence was singular enough had he simply walked by, for most of the men in England seemed to be under six feet, but he stopped and came back, looking intently at Hawkins who was carefully studying his tankard.

"Hawkins? Livesey Hawkins?" the man inquired tentatively. When Hawkins looked up in acknowledgement, the stranger's pudgy mug broke out into a broad grin. "It's Mr. Livesey Hawkins as I live and breath! I never thought I'd find you in a place like this!" he said as he vigorously shook Hawkins' hand. Hawkins' face broke into a grin of recognition as he shook the large gentleman's hand.

"Well, well, well, if it isn't Mr. Thomas Blessington! How do you do, sir?"

"I am quite well, thank you, very busy these days what with that gang of ruffs pillaging my beat. They're getting awfully cocky, but we'll get them in the end!"

"I am sure you will. By the way, this is my good friend, Dr. Andrew Collins," Hawkins said gesturing at me.

"It's a pleasure to meet you, sir!" Blessington shook my hand heartily until I winced, while pulling me close to whisper, "Stick close to Hawkins here. Maybe you can teach him some manners!" He slapped me on the back and laughed heartily.

"Collins," said Hawkins, "Mr. Blessington is a police constable. We've been acquainted for some time now."

"Indeed we have! Hawkins here is a brilliant fellow when it comes to riddles; I found that out the hard way!" Mr. Blessington paused to order a beer before continuing his narrative. "You see, I was with a group of gentlemen outside the Yard building one afternoon, and I was telling them a riddle. Well, none of the people in my group could solve it, but up walks Hawkins and asks if he may have a go. So I say 'Sure why not,' and tell him the riddle. Then what does he do? He off and solves it as quick as you please, making my friends all look like idiots. I was quite impressed I was. Since then, I've been trying to find the riddle that'd stump him."

"You have a gift for hyperbole, Mr. Blessington," smiled Hawkins. "However, you also have a gift for telling excellent riddles, and I look forward to hearing the one that will finally stump me."

"By Jove, listen to him carry on!" laughed Mr. Blessington as he prodded me in the ribs with his elbow. "Just you wait, and I'll get you yet!"

Mr. Blessington proved to be excellent company and kept us entertained with his many humorous stories. He was an incredibly cheerful person, and his good cheer was contagious. In Mr. Thomas Blessington's presence, the gloom of departing from Agatha lifted like fog in the sunshine. He was telling us about one of his misadventures when all of a sudden the room went dead silent. It was like a bar scene from an old Western movie; everyone looked at the door where a sinister-looking gentleman stood. The bartender trembled with fright, grabbed a bottle of whisky and a glass off the shelf, and took them to a table in the corner where a chessboard was set up. The man walked to the table and sat down, grimacing at all the people with his evil eyes. I half expected him to be wearing spurs. He picked up the bottle and poured himself a drink. Only when he had quaffed it did the people resume talking—quietly.

"Who's that guy? He looks mad about something," I whispered to Mr. Blessington.

"That is Eddie Grimsby. He's a big bully that one is."

"Really? So why is everyone afraid of him, if he's just a bully?"

"Because he's also the right hand of the greatest criminal mind in London—or so we believe. They haven't been able to get anything definite on him, but one of these days he'll slip up."

Grimsby looked up from his bottle and gestured to one of the men nearby to come to him. The man trembled as he did so, and Grimsby engaged him in a chess game.

"Ah, so he plays chess," Hawkins said. He rubbed his hands together, and his eyes were bright. I had a feeling I knew what he was thinking, and it didn't seem like a good idea.

"Yes, and he's good at it too, by George," replied Mr. Blessington. He likes to play the regulars at chess and humiliate them in as many moves as he wants."

"Has anyone ever beaten him?" I asked. Mr. Blessington stared at me incredulously for a moment before replying.

"Beat him? You can't beat him, he's too good! I've never seen him beat." The poor local man was laughed at mercilessly and finally dismissed by the amused Grimsby. The three of us watched him in silence for a moment.

"Someone ought to teach him a lesson," I said grimly.

"They should, but nobody's brave enough or good enough to. It's a real shame," replied Mr. Blessington.

I sighed and turned back to the bar to drink my beer when I noticed that Hawkins was gone. I turned around in dread and to my horror saw him heading toward Grimsby. Mr. Blessington followed my gaze and chuckled softly.

"Oh God!" I said as a feeling of panic rose within me. "He's going to get himself killed."

"He's a bloody fool he is," Blessington said with a hint of admiration in his voice, "but a brave fool at that."

"He's also the best chess player I have ever seen," I said.

"Is he now? Let's hope he's good enough."

From where I was standing at the bar, I could hear every word Hawkins and Grimsby said to each other. The fact that the room went silent helped. Apparently, nobody had ever challenged Grimsby before. Though it seemed such a trivial thing to be excited about, the tension in the room increased.

"I beg your pardon, sir," said Hawkins in his most polite tone, "I was wondering if you might allow me the honor of a game of chess." Grimsby leaned back in his chair, sizing up the slender, unimpressive figure of Hawkins.

"Well now, ain't you an audacious young Jack!" He sneered. "What makes you think someone with such tender years like yourself could beat me?"

"Sir, I assure you that my 'tender years' will prove more formidable than you think. In fact, I would be willing to bet that I will beat you in five moves or less," replied Hawkins calmly while setting a five-pound note on the table. Grimsby grinned and matched Hawkins' wager.

"All right," he said, "I'll bet that you won't even make it to five moves before I beat you. That should teach you not to be so damn cocky."

"Done!" Hawkins responded quietly as he sat down. Although his back was to me, I could picture the devilish gleam that was no doubt in his eyes.

Grimsby looked bored as the game commenced, but when Hawkins captured his queen on his second move, he looked a little less complacent. In fact, he seemed to get increasingly agitated. When Hawkins declared, "Checkmate!" on his fifth move, Grimsby jumped to his feet in unrestrained anger, upsetting the table in his agitation.

"Y-y-you, you scoundrel!" spluttered Grimsby in his rage. "You'll pay for this!" He stormed to the door, knocking people over in his anger. There was a moment of silence as Hawkins calmly stood and collected his two five-pound notes from among the scattered chess pieces, and then the room erupted with applause. I grinned and clapped for him. He broke out into a smile and bowed gracefully. When he returned to the bar, the bartender offered him a free drink.

"Thank you, sir," said Hawkins, "but my friend and I must be returning home, as it is getting late. Good day to you, Mr. Blessington." Hawkins grabbed his coat and hat and scuttled to the door. Amidst the clatter of the pub, we left—Hawkins beamed with quiet satisfaction.

"Well, that was stupid," I said to him as we climbed into a cab. "You could've gotten hurt. Then I would've had to clean up the stinkin' mess." To my surprise, Hawkins laughed. Starting as a low chuckle, it rose into a full-blown laugh that left him gasping for breath with streaming eyes and aching sides.

"I don't see anything funny about this," I said as sternly as I could. His laughter was contagious, and I laughed alongside him in spite of myself. We weren't able to compose ourselves until the cab pulled up outside our flat. I'm sure the cabby thought we were insane as we practically fell out of the vehicle gasping for breath.

We were greeted warmly by Mrs. Montgomery, who had missed us dearly during our absence. "It's good to see you two again, sirs. It was lonely around here without you," she offered as she took our coats for us.

"Thanks! It's good to be back." I said, shaking with suppressed laughter. She looked at me curiously and then at Hawkins who was grinning. She shook her head and went off down the hallway muttering something about us "drunken men." Hawkins and I looked at each other and burst out laughing again.

It was good to be home.

WE WERE AFFLICTED with rainy and drab weather for the rest of the month until November gave way to December. The morning of the first dawned cold and clear, and I learned of a Christmas tradition of Mrs. Montgomery's that Hawkins despised with his entire being: decking the halls for Christmas.

Hawkins was in a black mood that morning and played his violin with frustration. He threw down the instrument with impatience and paced the room while gnawing on his pipe. There was a soft knock on the door. Mrs. Montgomery entered with the mail and a rather lovely Christmas wreath. Hawkins ceased his agitated pacing and eyed the innocent decoration with disgust.

"What is that?" he asked with contempt.

Mrs. Montgomery replied sternly, "You know very well what it is, Mr. Hawkins. It's the wreath your sister sends down for you each December." She paused as Hawkins glowered at her and then continued with exasperation, "Must we go through this every year?"

"Go through what?" I asked.

"Decorating for Christmas," she replied. "I insist on decorating for the blessed holiday, and all I ask is for Mr. Hawkins here to decorate this room. But it's easier to move a mountain than it is for him to hang a simple wreath."

She paused for a moment, and Hawkins glowered at her murderously with his pipe in his mouth. She sighed and set the wreath down on the table.

"You just hang that wreath where you want to, and I will be back in a moment with more decorations." She left the door open, and went into the hallway and up into the attic.

Hawkins threw himself into a chair, scowling at the wreath all the while. After a few minutes, with only the clock on the mantelpiece daring to make noise, I mustered the courage to speak. "Uh, you know, Hawkins, I bet that wreath would look lovely hanging on the front of the door."

He frowned at it a few seconds longer before he replied. "You may be right, my dear Collins." A mischievous light crept into his eyes. He jumped up from his chair, walked to the mantelpiece, and picked up a short, thick knife. Although I had never known him to be violent, I felt scared as he fingered the weapon. He whirled and threw the knife at the open door with enough force to drive it through the wood almost up to the hilt. With a loud thud, it stuck in the exact center. Hawkins coolly walked over and inspected his handiwork, humming a sprightly tune. Casually, he hung the wreath over the knife and meticulously straightened it. After he finished, he picked up the mail and flopped back into his seat as if he had merely poked the fire.

Mrs. Montgomery bustled in a moment later, seeking the origin of the noise. I was still gripping the arms of my chair. She took one look at the wreath, my pale face, and Hawkins humming away in his chair before she sighed in exasperation and walked out of the room. Hawkins watched her over the top of the letter in his hand and snickered malevolently. If I had entertained any doubts as to his sanity before, they were reinforced at that moment.

After he had perused the mail for a moment longer, Hawkins stood and stretched languidly. I think one of his main pleasures in life was getting the better of our brave landlady, for he was in an infinitely better mood. He knew where to draw the line though, and he always made it up to her in some way after he had tormented her.

"Well, my dear fellow," he said pleasantly, "I think this room looks a little pathetic with only a wreath to brighten it. Let us see if we cannot bring some Christmas cheer in here." He turned to me with a bright smile on his face, but I was still gripping the arms of my chair. "Come, come, Collins, there's nothing to be afraid of. It's only a few decorations."

I scowled at him as I got up from my chair. Mrs. Montgomery returned with a box full of various decorations and fixed a look of scorn on Hawkins.

"I see you hung your wreath, Mr. Hawkins," she quipped.

"Yes, as a matter of fact, I did," he replied in a way that dared her to criticize him. She stared icily at him, left the box with us, and left the room. Then turning to me, Hawkins asked, "Well then, shall we?"

I AGREED TO HELP hang decorations under the condition that Hawkins would help me tidy the sitting room. After a lot of arguing that ended in a meaningless compromise, we both cleaned and decorated the sitting room with Mrs. Montgomery's help. I had recovered from my fright almost as quickly as Hawkins had recovered his good humor, and the day turned out to be quite pleasant.

After supper, a breathless Mr. Blessington and a man whom I had never seen before paid us a visit. The stranger had one of those faces that didn't seem capable of a smile and grey eyes that offered no warmth in their depths. He was almost the opposite of the cheerful Mr. Blessington in every way, for, in addition to his sallow face, he was built like a toothpick.

"Good evening, gentlemen," said Hawkins as he stood. "Please, have a seat."

"Thank you, Mr. Hawkins, that's very kind," replied Mr. Blessington. "This is Inspector Nigel Nelson of Scotland Yard, but I believe you two have met before." The inspector's perpetual scowl deepened, and Hawkins smiled ruefully. "He'd like to have a word with you, sir."

"Indeed, I would," said Inspector Nelson curtly.

"Ah, my dear Inspector, it has been awhile has it not? I must confess that I didn't expect to see you walk through my door ever again." Hawkins spoke politely, but his manner was haughty and condescending. The inspector stared ruthlessly, and his cheeks reddened with anger.

"It is only because of Mr. Blessington that I am here at all. I assure you that it is quite against my better judgment to consult you. The least you could do is behave civilly."

"Oh, my dear Inspector, have I offended you? I am so very sorry." His tone of voice indicated otherwise, of course, and he sat down in his armchair with a careless attitude. "Pray, take a seat and tell me how I may serve so noble a person as you."

"It is a delicate matter," Nelson said, glancing in my direction as he sat down.

"This is my friend, Dr. Collins, who is an incredibly upstanding citizen. If he is not allowed to stay in the room, then I fear you must also leave, which would make it very difficult for you to deliver your message."

I smiled and sat down in the chair next to Hawkins. Inspector Nelson fixed a derisive look at me until my smile melted from my face. The left corner of his mouth almost turned up slightly once he achieved his goal. He turned to Hawkins.

"Very well, I will trust your judgment."

"That would certainly be a first," Hawkins mumbled as he examined his nails closely.

Inspector Nelson cleared his throat and frowned determinedly. "Blessington tells me that the three of you had a run-in with Eddie Grimsby the other night."

"Indeed. And what of it, Inspector?"

"Well, we at the Yard have been trying to trace his boss and believe Grimsby to be a member of the gang of ruffians who have been pillaging London. However, they cover their tracks carefully each time, and we cannot find any evidence to convict them."

"Forgive me, Inspector," cut in Hawkins, "but I fail to see how this concerns me."

"I'm getting to that, sir. You have a particular gift for strategy, but does this ability extend toward the criminal classes?"

"Yes, I suppose so." Hawkins leaned back in his chair with his fingers laced behind his head.

"I have a task for you—a little problem to test your mind. How would you recommend we go about capturing

Grimsby's leader?"

"You could start by catching Grimsby and questioning him."

"It's been done before. He won't talk."

"Follow him, then."

"He shakes us off. Nothing has come of it."

"Then I see only one course of action. Are you familiar with the expression 'if you can't beat them, join them'?"

"What do you mean? Send a man in under cover to join the gang?"

"Precisely. Two men might be acceptable as well, but no more than that."

Inspector Nelson thought for a moment, the corner of his mouth curling up once more.

"Well, then, Mr. Hawkins, I can think of no one better suited for the job than you."

Hawkins straightened. I sat in stunned silence. "Why, surely you are joking," Hawkins pronounced.

"No, sir, I assure you I have never been more serious."

"But I have no experience with this sort of thing. There must be someone better suited than I."

"Experience-wise, there is no doubt that every man who works under me would be a better candidate for the job. But none of them have the wit or courage to beat Eddie Grimsby in a chess game. It pains me to say it, but I believe you are our only hope."

After a pause, Hawkins asked, "What must I do?"

"Hawkins! You aren't really thinking about doing this are you?" I asked incredulously.

"Hush, my dear Collins," he said to me and then turned back to inspector Nelson.

"It's simple enough. Join the gang. Tell us what you find out about them."

"For how long am I to do this?"

"As long as you can safely accomplish it. Use your discretion as to proper courses of action, and if you are as bright as you are acclaimed you should do well."

"Why, Inspector, I do believe that you may have inadvertently paid me a compliment."

Inspector Nelson glowered firmly at Hawkins. "This is an extremely dangerous mission. If you should fail, I will certainly not mourn you. However, you will not be going alone." His gaze rested on me, and I jumped with surprise.

"No. Absolutely out of the question, I cannot allow it." Hawkins protested.

"I will not engage you in this plot by yourself. If the doctor is willing, he will go with you," Inspector Nelson said. Hawkins shook his head firmly.

"Um, I don't mind," I interjected timidly, even though I really did mind.

"Collins, you are not going. I will not risk your life even if it means capturing every criminal in the world."

"Why Hawkins," I said, trying to imitate his attitude from earlier, "that might just be the nicest thing you have ever said to me."

"Oh, do be quiet," he said hotly. Blessington chuckled.

Inspector Nelson continued, "Look here, Hawkins, if we send the two of you there's a greater chance that at least one of you will survive."

"You inspire my confidence immensely with your reassuring words," said Hawkins dryly.

"Well? Besides, he's a doctor isn't he? He might come in handy."

"I'm not actually a doctor, I'm really a—" I responded as Hawkins interrupted me.

"I would hate to miss out on such an adventure, and if I must take someone with me I suppose it ought to be Collins," said Hawkins.

"Very well." Inspector Nelson rose to leave, but Blessington stayed seated. "Report to the Yard tomorrow morning at eight sharp, and we will relay everything else you need to know. Goodnight, gentlemen." He shot one last menacing glance around the room before exiting.

"Well, he's kind of . . . unpleasant." I said after a moment.

"He's really not all that bad once you get to know him," Blessington replied.

"Oh, Mr. Blessington, I really feel that you are incapable of thinking ill of anyone," Hawkins observed. Blessington beamed.

"Why does he hate you so much?" I asked.

"It is my firm belief that he despises all creatures, but with one notable exception. He adored his wife."

"Past tense? He doesn't like her anymore?"

"Indeed. By an odd coincidence, Mrs. Nelson was a friend of Mrs. Montgomery's and heard through her that I had advised some people regarding their domestic problems. She came to me and said that she had found herself in an impossible situation regarding her marital life. She could no longer tolerate her overbearing and scowling husband, and she wasn't sure what to do. I advised her to speak to her husband rather than me, but she didn't heed my advice. She committed an indiscretion that ended in divorce and married her lover. My name was mentioned somewhere, and Nelson has forever firmly believed that it is my fault that he is no longer married."

"Oh. That's pretty dumb. I mean if you told her to talk to her husband, but she acted against your advice, he really shouldn't blame you."

"Quite so."

"Well, I stand by what I said though, he's not so bad. He just takes a little extra effort to get along with is all," Blessington said.

"Yeah, he sure seems like it. I mean, does he ever smile?" I asked.

"I honestly don't believe his mouth to be capable of such an unusual act," Hawkins said.

Blessington stood to leave. "Well, gentlemen, I must be off. Good night to you, and good luck on your mission."

"I'll walk you to the door," I said.

Blessington and I went downstairs where he gathered his coat and hat. He paused before he left and looked at me reassuringly. I felt a knot form in my stomach. My desire to go with Hawkins had been an impulsive decision, and I now began to regret it.

"You'll do fine, both of you!" Mr. Blessington said to me. "I'll wager you two will be the best criminals in London before long." I was not reassured.

When I returned to the sitting room, Hawkins was in his chair with his legs criss-crossed beneath him, elbows on knees and fingertips pressed together. His eyes were bright with excitement as he contemplated this new adventure.

"Well, my dear Collins," he said, "it seems we must leave for awhile."

"I can't believe we're actually doing this. What are we thinking?"

"Collins, my friend, this is something I must do. You see, I am a mere knight in this chess game, and if I do not move, my life will have been in vain. I must do this. I am still averse to your presence, but I do appreciate you coming with me. I find that I am incomplete without my Watson. I give you my word that I will not let any harm come to you as long as there is breath in my body."

"Thanks, Hawkins. I didn't know you read Sherlock Holmes."

"I read only a portion of a story I found in a *Strand* magazine. It was quite uninteresting."

"You would say that."

I resumed my seat as he smiled, picked up his violin, and played a slow tune—a melancholic tune—that brought tears to my eyes. I could still hear him playing as I retired to bed that night, and I felt as though I was walking through a continual nightmare.

I dreamt that night that Hawkins and I stood on the edge of disaster together. We stared into the abyss, and he told me it was all going to be alright—just before we jumped. I woke up with my heart pounding just as we started to fall. After that, I couldn't sleep. I got up around five-thirty. I dressed, rehearsed the basic medical training I had, packed a small bag with the fixings for a first-aid kit, and went downstairs to meet my day. This was a big adventure, and I would be sharing it with my best friend. I determined to do everything in my power to prevent him from coming to harm, for life would be so much duller without Hawkins.

✳ CHAPTER IX

THERE ARE TIMES IN LIFE WHEN WE
need to stop and ask ourselves, What was I thinking?
Throughout the three weeks that I was a spy, I asked myself this
question frequently, but I never could find an answer. I was not
meant to be a spy, but I was enlisted as a cook for the gang, and I
also helped guard the headquarters. Hawkins did most of the
actual spy work, while I merely fit in and got on the good side of
many gang members.

We had no real difficulty in getting into the gang; in fact, the
hard part was disappearing from Mrs. Montgomery without her
knowing where we would be. Hawkins managed to partially
convince her that he had a fancy to see America and that I
would be traveling with him. We then slipped off to Scotland
Yard where we met the unhappy Inspector Nelson and received a
few final instructions. Hawkins wasn't given a disguise because
Grimsby had already seen his face, but I was given a fake
moustache, a pair of fake spectacles, and a fake name: Dr. William
P. Shadybrooke. We set out to find Eddie Grimsby and enter our
new life as criminals.

Grimsby was easy to locate. We found him mulling over a
bottle of brandy in the same pub as the day before. Hawkins was
the last person he wanted to see at that moment. As soon as he

laid eyes on him, he pulled out a gun. I thought that it would all end right there, but Hawkins was a smooth talker and loquaciously gabbed his way out of a sticky situation. In fact, the two of them were soon sitting at the table laughing over a half empty bottle of alcohol, while I stood behind Hawkins and tried not to look too scared.

"Eh, what's that? You're looking for work? Well the boss has a job open," Grimsby said. "It's not what you might call respectable, but it pays more than what you earn now I'll wager."

"Ah, I see. I'll take whatever work I can these days, especially if it shows up the infernal Scotland Yard." Hawkins apparently knew exactly what to say to this drunken ruffian for Grimsby brightened immensely.

"Scotland Yard, you say? You have a bone to pick with them?"

"Yes, but mainly with the ever-sour Inspector Nigel Nelson. He has paid me many insults, and I desire to settle the score."

"Well, that's good!" Grimsby sat up and slapped the table joyously. "We have a common enemy! But what of your friend there? You look like a man of your word, but he looks like a coward."

My cheeks reddened. I was about to speak up and defend myself, but Hawkins cut in before I could.

"Ah yes, he is a little timid, but the law has been none too friendly to him either. I would not recommend him for any criminal work, but he is an excellent doctor."

"A doctor, you say? Well, I suppose we can find something for him to do. Can he cook?"

"Superbly."

"Good, bring him along then. What's his name?"

"I am Dr. William P. Shadybrooke," I said.

"Shadybrooke and Hawkins," Grimsby said musingly. He studied the two of us for a moment and stood up. "Well, come with me, and we'll see what the boss thinks."

Hawkins stood, and we followed Grimsby out. Grimsby was incredibly bow-legged, but he walked remarkably quickly in spite of this. Hawkins had no trouble keeping up with him, but I was forced to remain a pace or two behind. I had the opportunity to study our guide better now that we were out of the dimly lit pub, and he made quite a sight. He was a little taller than Hawkins. Though he couldn't have been too much older than I, he looked well into his forties. His hair was thin and sat in an untidy mess on his head. His face turned toward me a few times; it was tanned and heavily lined with a layer of stubble on his chin and cheeks. His clothing consisted of a faded green jacket, a reddish waistcoat, tan breeches, gaiters, purple cravat, and a brown bowler hat. None of these articles were in good condition, and all were filthy. They seemed to suit him admirably, adding to his bully-like appearance.

Grimsby led us on a long walk through the maze of London streets. Most of the time I had no idea where we were. We passed through streets clogged with horse-drawn vehicles, small side streets with only a couple of pedestrians, large villas with maids scrubbing the front steps clean, small duplexes (they called them semidetached houses), and other curious sights. After an hour or so of weary trudging, we came to a row of docks along the Thames. Grimsby headed for a warehouse at the end of the dock and knocked boldly on the door. A gruff voice on the other side asked for a password.

"Password? Toby, you old coot, we don't have a password! Let me in, or I'll knock a hole in your skull," Grimsby barked. I heard chuckling on the other side of the door, which was opened by a scruffy-looking elderly man with yellow hair.

"Aye now, wot's all teh fuss, Eddie? I 'as just 'avin' a bit o' fun with 'ee," Toby snickered.

"Get out of it, you old drunkard." Grimsby shoved Toby and led us into the warehouse.

The building's interior was filled with wooden crates of all sizes and the roughest-looking lot of men I had ever seen. They were stacking crates. Grimsby led us through the crowd to the back of the room where there was a staircase leading up to a balcony. At the top were a couple of office doors. We headed to the first door.

Entering the office was like walking into another world. Where the warehouse was decorated only by its occupants, the office was richly decorated with various tapestries and pieces of priceless artwork. There wasn't much furniture—a stove in one corner, a beautiful desk, two chairs in front of the desk, and a large safe in the corner. A man was sitting behind the desk, and Hawkins stopped short when he saw him. The man looked surprised.

"You? What are you doing here?" the man growled. Grimsby looked from the unknown man's face to Hawkins' face and back several times.

"You two know each other?" he asked.

"Yes, I'm ashamed to say we do. I had hoped to never see this gentleman again."

"Hawkins?" I asked.

"This man was once called my brother, although he is in actuality not related to me at all. He is Agatha's older brother," Hawkins explained.

"Agatha's brother, not yours, and don't you ever forget it. Now what is it you want? I am a busy man, so be brief." The unknown man said.

"He's here for a job, sir," Grimsby interjected. "They both are." The man behind the desk turned his gaze on me as if he was seeing me for the first time. He looked elderly—brown hair streaked with gray and a face lined with years. His green eyes were bright with intelligence, and he was dressed like a gentleman, unlike the other men I had seen. Overall, he reminded me of Charles Dickens' Ebenezer Scrooge.

"And who the devil are you?" He yelled at me. I jumped a little, and my voice broke when I replied.

"I, uh, I'm Dr. William P. Shadybrooke."

"Hm, he's an absolute coward, Grimsby. See how his hands shake even as we speak? There's no blood for crime in him. What possessed you to bring him?"

"Well, he's a doctor, sir. I thought maybe we could use one, especially after what happened to old Doc Peters. Besides, he can cook too."

"You may be right, for once. Fine, we will keep him." He turned to me with a condescending look. "You sir, my name is Professor Stephen Davies. As long as you work for us, you will report to Eddie Grimsby or me, and you will do as you're told. If you try anything—original—it will be the last move you ever make. Do you understand?"

"Y-yes, sir." I stuttered. Davies looked disgusted for a moment.

"He's an American on top of everything. How revolting." His gaze turned to Hawkins. "Now then, give me one good reason why I should hire you."

"Because you can't do without me." Hawkins replied coolly.

"Oh? And why pray tell is that?"

"You plan all of your raids yourself, correct?"

"Yes. And they are all successful too."

"Successful is one word, I would be more inclined to call them pathetic."

"Pathetic? And I suppose you think you can do better, is that it?"

"Of course not; I know I can do better."

"Humph. I gave you the choice to work for me before, but you refused. Why the change of heart?"

"Oh, you know how it is when you get tired of being on the good side of the law." Hawkins' words apparently had some bite to them, and Davies looked somewhat uncomfortable. "I tire of strategizing for the ungrateful patrons of London, and I simply wish to find work that is more challenging."

"Fine, I'll hire you as well. But that doesn't mean I trust you or even like you."

I heard Hawkins whisper under his breath, "You'd be a fool if you did." But to Davies, he said, "Excellent!"

Davies warned, "If you dare try anything on me, I'll serve you ill, Jeremy. Do you quite understand?" He shook his finger at Hawkins to emphasize his point.

"Absolutely."

"Good. Eddie, take them down and show them the ropes."

"Yes sir," answered Grimbsy. Eddie took us out of the office, and back down the stairs to the warehouse floor. "Alright gents," he said to the roomful of men. "These are the new recruits. Be nice to them now." A chorus of rough laughter went up through the room, and I smiled nervously. And so we were initiated into the gang.

I am ashamed to say that I was a rather timid gang member, and I was never trusted enough to go on raids. This was preferable for me, for I knew my conscience would never let me do anything illegal. Hawkins, however, planned every raid and soon earned his brother's trust. He seemed to be enjoying our adventure immensely, and there were times I wondered whose side he was on.

I remained at the warehouse all day every day—on call, so to speak—and I seldom saw Hawkins because he was always busy. The only time we were ever able to talk was at night, and we were usually too tired to say much. Spying was stressful, and I wasn't sure how much more of it I could take. Hawkins assured me that he was making progress. One night he came in the warehouse looking like a beaten man and plopped down on a crate next to me where I was sitting away from the other members.

"You know, Collins," he whispered to me, "I will be glad when this whole damned business is over."

"I thought you were enjoying yourself."

"Davies and Grimsby found a member of the gang who was suspected of being a spy. They asked me to murder him in order to prove my loyalty."

I sat up a little straighter on my crate and looked where I knew Hawkins was in the darkness.

"What did you do?" I asked. Knowing what the answer would likely be.

"I shot him." He paused for a moment as if waiting for me to respond. When I didn't say anything, he continued. "I had to do it; it was either him or me. Oh, but the look on his face—it shall haunt me the rest of my days. Collins, I am close to nailing Davies and his entire gang, but I just need a little more time to gather my evidence."

"What do you want me to do?"

"Nothing, my friend; they are already suspicious. I fear if you try anything you may come to harm. Just be ready to run when I tell you."

"Will do. Hey, Hawkins?"

"Yes?"

"Do you think I'm a coward?"

He chuckled softly. "My dear fellow, there is a difference between cowardice and kindness. You may not have the courage to face a ruthless bully, but you have something even Davies himself lacks."

"What's that?"

"A caring heart and a sound conscience. When the time comes for you to be brave, I have little doubt that you will come through brilliantly."

After that, I saw even less of Hawkins. I had no idea what he was planning, but I suspected that it boded ill for Davies and his gang. The days went by slowly, but I did have one companion in the warehouse all day: Toby. Since he was in charge of guarding the warehouse during the day, Toby often became bored. He was rather garrulous and talked to me for hours on end. He knew a lot about the gang. I asked some imprudent questions, and he was proud to share his expertise.

Through Toby, I learned more about our leader, Davies. His actual name was William Peter Bartholomew Hawkins, and he had possessed so much animosity toward his adopted brother that he eventually changed his name to Stephen Elliot Davies while he was still young. He had been a respected scientist and professor of science once, but crime was more to his liking. The warehouse belonged to him, and he was known to be in the shipping and storage business. The public was told that his business was inherited or else he might still be a professor. He had the sympathy and respect of his peers, who thought him noble for giving up his dreams to prevent his father's work from vanishing. The members of the gang were on his payroll as simple workmen, but they were criminals. This was all Toby knew, and I remained full of questions. However, I would have to wait to ask Agatha and Hawkins.

THREE WEEKS HAD ELAPSED since the day I had become a spy. I wasn't treated poorly, but, at first, I was ignored by everyone except Hawkins and Toby. Most of the men considered me to be a coward, but I was also a great listener and let a few of them talk through their troubles. Besides that, I could cook rather well— thanks to Mrs. Montgomery—and I earned their respect slaving over the warehouse's woodstove that doubled as a cooking stove. They nicknamed me Dr. Mutton, and I almost began to enjoy being the gang's cook and counselor. But on December 19, things abruptly changed.

The day started fairly normal and progressed as other days had before it. The entire gang was out on a raid, and I was once again left alone with Toby. I had seen Hawkins earlier that morning. He told me that things were coming to a head that night, and I needed to trust him completely.

Around six o'clock that evening, while bandaging Toby who had cut his hand open while whittling a piece of wood, Davies approached and asked to have a word with me in his office. I sensed something wrong but had no option but to follow Davies upstairs. When Grimsby closed the door behind me, I felt like a trapped animal.

"Dr. Shadybrooke, how are you this evening?" Davies asked as he sat down at his desk. I stood before the desk, and Grimsby stood behind me.

"Fine, how're you?"

"I must say, I have been better. You see, it has come to my attention that there is a spy in the gang, and I have been rather pressed to find him." He calmly pulled out a revolver and started cleaning it.

"A spy? That's not good. I hope you find him." I turned to leave, but Grimsby blocked my path. I debated knocking him over and running for it, but Davies' cold voice stopped me.

"Leaving so soon, Dr. Collins? Ah, so that is your name!" I

turned around slowly, and Davies smiled maliciously. "Have a seat doctor. I have a few questions for you."

I sat down. Davies got up and walked around the desk. He sat on its edge just in front of me and set his revolver next to him. Grimsby moved behind my chair.

"It seems rather odd, doesn't it doctor?" he asked.

"Huh?"

"I mean that such a shrimp as you should be capable of spying on me. I can see the genuine fear in your eyes, and I don't think you are dangerous at all."

"Oh well, you better believe it. I, uh, I'll see you get what's coming to you." I tried to sound brave, and Davies laughed.

"My, aren't we valiant! Now then, tell me who your confederate is."

I remained silent and stared out the office window beyond Davies.

"Ah, so that's how it will be, eh? Grimsby, would you please knock the noble sentiments out of this fellow."

"I'd be happy to, sir!"

Grimsby came around in front of me and punched me a couple times in the head. I felt the blood run down my face and thought my nose was broken. I didn't say anything.

"Are you working with my adopted brother?" I remained silent. "Ah, but your silence speaks louder than anything you could say. Tell me, where is he tonight?"

I held my tongue and Grimsby proceeded to encourage me to speak. I fought back this time, but they easily overpowered me and tied my hands and legs to the chair.

"Wish we had thought of that sooner," Grimsby said as he rubbed where I had kicked him. I smiled with satisfaction.

For half an hour Davies questioned me, and for half an hour I kept my mouth shut. By the end of that time, Grimsby had fairly beaten me to a pulp. I wished I would pass out.

"Sir, this is pointless. He's clammed up." Grimsby rubbed his sore fists and scowled at my bloody face.

"Yes, I suppose you're right." Davies picked up his revolver.

"He has rather more loyalty than courage. I fear that this is his downfall. Now then, doctor, this is your last chance. Will you tell us anything and save your life?"

"Yeah, here's something for you." I was surprised by how hoarse my voice sounded, and Davies leaned in closer. I shouted, "Go to hell, jerk!"

Davies stood and sighed, "It is such a pity, is it not?"

Davies raised the revolver to my head. I steeled myself for the blow I was sure would follow. Just as he was squeezing the trigger, the door burst open, someone barged in, and Grimsby was thrown against Davies. The gun went off while they were scrambling to recover their balance, and I felt the bullet hurtle past my head and strike the wall. I looked to the new arrival and was relieved to see Hawkins. In his flashing eyes was a look of fierce anger that I had never seen before. Grimsby was the first to get to his feet, but Hawkins knocked him back down with a savage blow to the head. Davies was about to raise his gun, but Hawkins pinned him hard against the wall.

"Now wait, wait, you wouldn't kill your own brother would you?" Davies pleaded while struggling to free himself. Hawkins tightened his grip around the professor's throat and spoke through clenched teeth.

"You would be so despicable as to say that, wouldn't you? Let me tell you something. If you ever try to harm Collins again, I will have no compunction in killing you." After retrieving the revolver, he knocked out Davies and hurried over to untie me from my chair.

"Collins, my dear fellow, are you alright?" he asked.

"Yeah, I'll be alright. I just need an ice pack and maybe a band-aid or two. You wouldn't happen to have any Ibuprofen would you?"

"My dear fellow, you are speaking nonsense. They must have hit you quite hard. Wait here a moment. We haven't much time, but we have time enough for this." He hurried over to where Davies lay and took his keys. Hawkins went to the safe, unlocked it, and pulled out all the papers, stuffing them into a leather satchel.

I was starting to recover my senses, and I heard noise coming from outside the office.

"What're you doing? What's going on?" I asked. He stuffed the last few papers into his satchel, closed it carefully, and hurried to me.

"I haven't time to explain right now, but that would be the gang returning. We must leave, now. Can you walk?"

"I think so."

"Good. Can you swim?"

"Swim? I never learned to swim."

"That is unfortunate. This is your chance to learn. Come with me."

I heard raised voices and feet on the stairs. Hawkins helped me to my feet, and the room spun around for a moment. Hawkins urged me to hurry—I think he carried me to the window. There was pounding on the door, and I saw Davies regaining consciousness. Hawkins opened the window. Water was below us. He put his arm around my chest. As the door broke open, he jumped out with me in tow. The water rushed up, engulfing us in its icy depths.

The cold water restored my senses, but it did nothing to help the fact that I didn't know how to swim. The impact had broken Hawkins' grip on me, and for a moment I was sure I was going to drown. The salt water stung my eyes. I couldn't figure out which way was up. I felt a hand grab the collar of my shirt and pull me to the surface.

"Come on, Collins, the shore is just ahead," Hawkins shouted and helped me along. I looked up at the window we had just exited. We were almost abreast of it. I saw people leaning out of the window; because it was dark, I couldn't tell who they were. One of them shouted something, and they all disappeared. I felt the ground beneath my feet and stood up.

"They are coming, Collins. We must be swift." Hawkins motioned to me to hurry.

We started running, and he made sure I was ahead of him the whole time. The urgency in Hawkins' voice and actions lent me wings, and I sprinted. The gang had just come out of the warehouse a moment after we started running, but when I looked back I noticed that we were a ways ahead of them.

"We have to get out of the open, there is an alley—" I heard a gunshot. Hawkins hit the ground with a loud cry. With dread, I stopped, looked back, and saw him holding his right leg. He shouted at me to keep going.

"I'm not leaving you!" I dropped to my knees beside him and quickly examined the wound. The bullet had struck his calf and exited out the front of his leg. The men were close, but I knew I had to get Hawkins' leg to stop bleeding before I did anything else. I quickly took off my cravat, a gift from Mrs. Montgomery, and tied it around Hawkins' leg. He winced as I tightened it, but it was sufficient to control the bleeding.

"Collins, they'll be on us in a moment. You must leave me here. I can distract them while you escape."

"I told you, I'm not leaving you." I helped him up. He couldn't walk, so I threw him over my shoulder. Struck by inspiration, I ran toward the water. The gang was practically on us. They seemed to be out of bullets, for none of them shot at us. I determined to jump into the river to escape. Just as I was about to do so, I heard a constable's whistle behind me.

"Finally!" Hawkins said.

I discerned a band of policemen in the gaslights who surrounded the gang. I set Hawkins down on the ground, supporting him so he wouldn't fall, as one of the constables walked up to us—Mr. Blessington. Dizziness washed over me, and the beating I had been subjected to caught up to me. I had been running on adrenaline. Now that the crisis was over, I wasn't sure I could remain conscious.

"Hello, sirs! It looks like you two have had quite a time," Blessington said cheerfully. About to respond, I passed out. As I fell to the ground, the last thing I heard was Hawkins yell my name, "Collins!"

✳ CHAPTER X

WHEN I REGAINED CONSCIOUSNESS, I was lying on the bed in my room on Montague Street, every bone in my body aching. My various cuts had been neatly bandaged. A basin of water and some medical supplies rested on my nightstand—evidence of the care I had received. I was in considerable pain, but I could sit up and even walk. I threw on my robe and gingerly went downstairs. I paused outside the sitting room door for a moment, listening to the voices inside. The wreath Hawkins had hung still decorated the front of the door, and it was comforting to see it. I entered the sitting room.

Hawkins was sitting in his chair by the fire and looked up as I entered. Inspector Nelson and Mr. Blessington were seated opposite him, and both of them stared openly at my bruised complexion.

"Hey, guys." I said, noticing that my voice still sounded hoarse.

"I didn't expect to see you up and about so soon, Collins," Hawkins said.

"I expect he looks worse than he feels," Inspector Nelson said blandly.

I went to the looking glass on the wall and jumped a little when I saw my reflection. Both of my eyes were black and blue, but not swollen, and my face was pale where it wasn't bruised. My upper lip was cut, and a clean piece of linen was wrapped around my forehead. I observed with satisfaction though that, although it was swollen, my nose had not been broken. My appearance was ghastly, but I couldn't help but laugh when I saw myself. Blessington joined in heartily, and Hawkins chuckled a little. Nelson's mouth twitched.

"Well, don't I look great. If I had known that I looked like this, I might've put a mask on before coming in." I went to the desk and sat down.

"You gave us quite a scare, you did," Blessington declared. "When you passed out I mean. It seems as though you took quite a beating."

"Yeah, they knocked me about pretty good. It's all a little foggy. What exactly happened?"

Hawkins responded, "Throughout our stay in Professor Davies' gang, I had been secretly informing Scotland Yard of developments and giving my advice on how to proceed. This was difficult at first, but it became easier as I earned Davies' trust and began laying plans to capture the gang."

"They aren't a large lot, but they are cunning," Inspector Nelson added with his usual scowl.

"Indeed, but they are not altogether infallible." Hawkins replied. "Anyway, a few days ago, Davies asked me to plan the most daring raid his gang would ever attempt. He wanted to plunder London Tower."

"What's that?" I asked. The three men stared at me in surprise.

"Why, it is only the home of the crown jewels, sir. A very tempting place for a robber, but it takes a great feat to plunder it," Blessington said.

"I always thought London Tower was the Big Ben clock tower."

"Oh no, my dear fellow, you have it quite wrong. I will show you London Tower when we both are well," Hawkins said. "I would be lying if I said I did not enjoy planning the heist of the century. It presented quite an intellectual treat, and my plan was absolutely foolproof. Davies was quite pleased with it, but what he did not know is that I had already informed Scotland Yard of the heist. A band of constables would be waiting to apprehend the thieves as they committed the crime.

"My plans changed when I discovered that Davies intended to send only his principal gang members on the London Tower raid. I realized that the only chance we would have of nabbing the fiends would be to trap them in their lair like so many rats. I left for Scotland Yard in order to discuss the matter with Nelson. I had intended to return to the warehouse to get you before matters fell out, but I was detained at Scotland Yard. When I returned, Toby informed me that Davies and Grimsby had taken you upstairs. I immediately went to the office, and the band who robbed London Tower returned shortly after this. They were alerted by the gunshot, but it was the sounds of a struggle that brought the entire gang upstairs. The rest I believe you know. We escaped into the Thames and were eventually saved by the impeccable timing of the London constabulary."

"But wait, I remember that you emptied the safe in Davies' office. What did you put in that bag?" I asked.

Hawkins smiled. "I knew the safe to be full of documents of an incriminating nature, and I knew they would be useful. Thanks to the impermeability of leather, the documents survived our swim. They were taken into the custody of Inspector Nelson last night."

"Ah. So did you get the whole gang?"

"No, I'm afraid we couldn't get them all. We did get the principal members, including Davies, and a few others. It is unlikely that the other ruffians are still in England," Inspector Nelson said.

"If they ever do show their faces again, we'll give them good reason to leave," Blessington said with a laugh.

"Speaking of leaving, we must be off. Good day to you, gentlemen." Inspector Nelson stood and walked to the door with Blessington on his heels. Before leaving, he paused and turned back to us with a humbled look on his face. "I just wanted to say, good work, gentlemen. Your performance was exemplary."

"Why, thank you, Inspector. It was a pleasure," Hawkins said, obviously enjoying the Inspector's discomfiture.

"Yes, well, don't get any ideas about joining the criminals. There is a place for ruffians like that, and it is already occupied." Having thus reasserted his harsher side, the Inspector whirled on his heel and whisked out the door. Blessington smiled, bowed slightly, and followed his scowling friend outside. I heard the front door shut, and Hawkins chuckled.

"We must have done remarkably well to receive such high praise from that man," he said.

"It was a change if nothing else. I don't think I'm suited to be a criminal though."

"Oh, I think you could if you really wanted. However, I recommend you stay on this side of the law. It may not be so lucrative, but your conscience will surely reward you for your good behavior."

"Yeah, I bet. Hey, um, thanks for saving my life last night. I wasn't sure I was going to make it out of that one alive."

"Well, I could not have let them kill you, my dear fellow. Agatha and Mrs. Montgomery would have never forgiven to me." He paused and continued in a softer tone. "I must admit that I myself would not have been completely unaffected as well."

"Thanks, Hawkins."

He nodded and resumed speaking in his flippant air. "I must apologize for not entirely keeping my promise, though, for despite my best efforts you did in fact become injured."

"Ah well, I'll be ok. It's not the first time that I've had the crap kicked out of me."

"Dare I ask what 'crap' is?"

"Uh, well I think it would be better if you didn't."

"Ah, I see."

"So what happened to the crown jewels?"

"The gang had successfully stolen them, thanks to my brilliant scheme, but the jewels were safely returned to London Tower."

"One more question. Did you know that Davies was the leader of the gang before we saw him?"

"I had suspected he might be. I knew that he had turned to a life of crime, but I had not heard of him for some years. He is a bitter man. However, he is safely brooding behind a set of bars at the moment, so we need not worry about him."

After having satisfied myself on these points, I made good use of the sofa in hopes that it would alleviate some of my sufferings. Before I could become settled, Mrs. Montgomery announced that Dr. Alasdair Fitzpatrick had come to call. Hawkins groaned.

"Who's that?" I asked.

"He's the gentleman who treated your wounds, sir. Shall I show him up?" I noticed Mrs. Montgomery was smiling a little more broadly than usual, and her cheeks had a reddish tinge.

"Yeah, show him in," I said. Hawkins shot me an icy look, and Mrs. Montgomery left the room. I waited until the door closed behind her before addressing my friend.

"Hey, is it just me, or is she acting a little strange?"

"Dr. Fitzpatrick is a very good friend of Mrs. Montgomery's."

"I see. Is he a good guy?"

"I suppose so. He is also quite Scottish."

"Scottish? I thought Fitzpatrick was an Irish name?"

"It is, but you will have to discuss his lineage with him."

There was a knock on the door, followed by the entrance of a rotund, elderly gentleman. He had fading red hair, complete with a beard and sideburns, a pointed nose, and twinkling eyes. He smiled cheerfully at us and set his bag on the sideboard.

"Good mornin' genl'men," said Fitzpatrick.

His accent was pretty thick, but thankfully I could still understand him. "Good morning, doctor," I said. Hawkins stared at the carpet with a vacant expression.

"Well, laddie, ye look a grand sight better than last night. Aye, ye were a wee bit fright'ning, and Eleanor, stout-hearted lass as she is, narly feented at the sight o' ye."

"Eleanor?" I looked at Hawkins for help, but he smiled and

continued to stare at the floor.

"Aye, Eleanor. Eleanor Montgomery is her nem, and what a bonny lass she is too." He winked at me, and I couldn't help but smile at the thought that our dear landlady had an admirer.

"Oh, right. I never really knew her first name. She's a neat lady."

"Neat, ye say? Well I suppose she is rather tidy."

"I mean neat as in cool. Oh, never mind."

He sat down and smiled with a somewhat whimsical expression. "Aye, I remember ween we ferst met just five wee years ago. I narly ran her o'er with me horse as she was crossin' the road."

"That's terrible!"

"It almos' was laddie, but she was alus quick to forgive." He took out a worn-looking wooden pipe, lit it, sending a plume of blue smoke into the air. "She stole me heart that day, and I canna say she ever gave it back."

"Why don't you marry her?"

"Marry? Nay, I could'na marry her. I'm not the young lad I once was, and she isna' a lass either. Nay, we ken enjoy each other's coompany, and tha'll do, lad, tha'll do."

"You two would be a great couple."

"Aye, perhaps ye are right there, but I didna' come here to talk about me love life." He stood to grab his bag off the table and pulled a few instruments out of it. "Now then, who's ferst?"

Dr. Fitzpatrick wasn't a bad doctor by any means, and I learned a lot about medical techniques from him. He had been educated in England, but he knew a few Scottish cures as well. He examined me first and found that I was healing nicely and in no danger as long as I took care of myself. He then tried to examine Hawkins' leg wound, and if I hadn't pleaded with Hawkins to cooperate, the poor Scotsman would've found himself in dire straits. I recalled that Hawkins detested doctors, but I never realized to what extent until that day.

Dr. Fitzpatrick, having finished his professional work, gave me a few pointers for taking care of my friend—one of the main ones was to not let him move around too much—and then left us. I accompanied him to the top of the stairs and stopped him before he descended. "Hey, you know I bet Mrs. Montgomery would really appreciate it if you dropped by more. You might try to bring flowers too. I bet that would help."

"I du'no lad, she might thenk me a knave, and I couldn'a have that."

"A knave? Nah, I bet she'd love it. It couldn't hurt to try anyway."

"Aye, I guess so. Well, I'll be seein' ye later on. Tek care of your friend now, 'e's a good lad but none too keen for me."

I watched him descend the stairs and returned to the sitting room. Hawkins was standing at the window, leaning on his cane.

"You know, I'm pretty sure your leg would benefit from rest more than motion." I said as I plopped down on the couch. My head had started to throb a little, and a few hours of peaceful oblivion sounded inviting.

"Perhaps, but I need to move at the moment. It is far more painful to sit still than it is to move around," he replied quietly.

"Bored? Well I'm sure we can find something for you to do." I said.

"I doubt it."

I sighed wearily. He was in one of his moods, and I knew it was best to let him be. It had started raining heavily, and the wind blew the moisture against the window pane violently. I watched the droplets race down the glass until my eye lids closed wearily. The clock on the mantelpiece kept up a steady rhythm, and it nicely complemented the erratic one of the rain.

"What does it feel like, I wonder?" Hawkins' voice snatched me from the arms of sleep, and I roused myself drowsily.

"Huh?" I yawned. "What does what feel like?"

"Love."

"Love? You've never been in love?"

"No."

"I'm sorry, but that's kind of sad."

"What is passion, Collins? I have heard rumors of it, seen it written on others' faces. But when I tried to pursue it and experience it for myself, it always escaped me. I've come close with music, so very close, but never close enough."

"But I've heard you play your violin with such emotion. You've made me cry a few times."

"I have watched some of the world's greatest musicians, and I envy their passion. I learned how to imitate them in the hope that it would aid me, but I was mistaken."

"Oh." I wasn't sure what to say.

"Look at the people on the street, Collins." I rose and walked to the window. "What do you see?"

The rain was still falling heavily in the street, and there were very few people out. A young boy was huddled on a doorstep with a kitten, a woman with an uncooperative umbrella called for a cab while her skirts rapidly became soaked, and an elderly man in an overcoat stood next to the street lamp to brave the weather. There was nothing remarkable about these people. I couldn't see a connection. "Well, I see a boy, a lady, and a man. All three are fighting the rain in one way or another. What do you see?"

"I see a growing shoot, a falling blossom, a withering weed. Three boats set adrift in a vast ocean, and all are floating to their end. The only difference between them is the stage of the journey they are in." He paused for a moment before continuing. "We are all boats in a sea, battered and beaten by the waves of life and guided by our hearts. But I am different. My heart does not guide me; it only serves to circulate the blood through my body, and therefore my head must take over where my heart does not. You once said I was gifted with a great intellect, but you were mistaken. I am cursed with a brain where my heart should be. I do not know what it is to feel passion. I have never been driven by anger—only by the conviction that I know I should be upset. Sadness is my solitary companion.

"You are fortunate, my friend. I can see the emotions you've experienced painted into your face like a great work of art. There is love in the brightness of your eyes, pain that you have suffered in the lines of your brow, and even evidence of past anger in the curve of your mouth. My canvas is blank and empty; my path through the sea is straight and predictable. I know that I shall die alone, and it frightens me that I am not frightened." Hawkins turned from the window and limped toward his bedroom. His violin was sitting on the couch. He stopped next to it and picked it up with a trembling hand. He hobbled to the sitting room door and hurled the instrument down the stairs before going into his room and closing the door behind him. I remained where I was with a feeling of pity for my friend as I listened to the violin strike the stairs multiple times before landing at the bottom.

The woman in the street had finally managed to catch a cab, but the man and the boy had remained. A growing shoot and a withering weed being battered by a downpour. They too eventually left the scene, being replaced by others who also left while I stood watching, and the sky gradually grew dark on the sea of uncertainty.

✳ CHAPTER XI

D UE TO INSPECTOR NELSON'S DILIGENCE, Davies was to be tried on December 21, just three days after our return from spying. The rest of the gang that had been captured would be tried and sentenced later that day.

Hawkins had become more silent and brooding since our return, and I was concerned for his well-being. I wasn't sure what was wrong with him. As his friend, it was my responsibility to find out what was on his troubled mind. I had a chance to ask him just after we received the letter saying when the trial was.

"Hawkins," I said.

He stared into the fire vacantly and barely troubled to respond. "Hmm?"

"You seem, well, I mean, uh, well, you're depressed."

"Astounding. However did you come to that conclusion?" he retorted sarcastically.

"I'm worried about you," I said softly. He stirred slightly but still didn't look up at me. "What's on your mind? Maybe I can help."

"I have always been guided by my head, and never by my heart. Many think me cold and unemotional, and they are right. I am, and I know I am. I have never regretted my past actions, at least not until recently." He paused, and I noticed that his hands were shaking.

"Is this about the guy Davies had you kill?"

Hawkins broke down completely and hid his head in his hands while he sobbed quietly.

"Oh, Collins, I wish I had never agreed to spy on that gang! I didn't even know that poor man's name," he said between sobs.

"I didn't think something like this would affect you so much. You're always so cynical."

"When Agatha was a year old, I found a litter of kittens in the barn one afternoon. Their mother was nowhere to be found, so I brought them into the house. My father was very angry, and he forced me to watch while he drowned them. He said it would teach me not to grow attached to vermin. My worst nightmares have always ended with running water and meowing kittens."

"Oh." I felt moved by my friend's sorrow, but I wondered why he should be so affected by death. A thought then occurred to me. "Hawkins, were you there when your mother died?"

He grew silent but continued to tremble, and I feared I had been insensitive with my questions.

"Yes."

So that was it then. He wouldn't say anything more, and I decided not to press the issue.

Hawkins controlled his emotions. He stared at the fire silently the rest of the day. I decided it was better to let him sit for the moment, and I would act if necessary. His aversion toward death seemed to explain a few things, such as his protectiveness of those he was close to, but it still puzzled me that he should have such a deep regard for life and yet be so cynical. It didn't make any sense, but at least I understood him a little better.

The two days before the trial rushed by, and December 21 was upon us. My injuries were healing. Although I wasn't at my best, I felt better. Hawkins' leg was still in a bad state, and Dr. Fitzpatrick had done everything but tie Hawkins down in order to keep him from walking on it. I intended to go to the trial alone that morning and was surprised when Hawkins limped out of his room, fully dressed and ready to go.

"You're not planning on going to the trial are you?" I asked.

"Of course, I am going, what would make you think differently?" He leaned against the mantelpiece heavily and caught his breath.

"Are you sure it's a good idea? I mean, do you really think it's wise of you?"

"Wise? No, I think not. However, it is necessary."

"Necessary? It's necessary that you rest that leg of yours so it can heal."

He turned to me with a look of impatience. "Collins, please, you worry far too much. I will be perfectly fine as long as I can find my damn pipe! Ah, here it is. Are your ready? We must depart."

There was no arguing with him, and the two of us left in plenty of time for the trial. The courthouse was filling up rapidly when we arrived. Inspector Nelson and Mr. Blessington met us.

"Good morning, gentlemen!" Blessington bellowed cheerfully. "The greatest criminal mind of our era will finally be brought to justice for his actions, and we have you two to thank for it."

Hawkins stared at the ground with a slight smirk on his face, and I shook hands with Blessington.

"Yes, we are very grateful." Inspector Nelson said with a scowl. I questioned his sincerity.

The trial began on time, with the honorable Judge John Harrowitz presiding. A tough-looking British jury looked toward the calm-looking Davies as the clerk read the crimes he was accused of. Davies stood almost proudly in front of the court and cast a defiant look around the room until his eyes rested on Hawkins. The two of them exchanged harsh stares across the courtroom throughout the entire trial.

It seemed that Davies had his start as a criminal from an early age, although there was no official record of this. The first time he was caught, he was charged with petty larceny and sentenced to six months of imprisonment. He was just fourteen at the time. After that, he determined never to get caught again. He kept a diary of his crimes, which was among the documents Hawkins retrieved from the safe and proved to be damning evidence, especially since it was written in his own handwriting. Davies had fought his way to the top of the underworld of criminals and set himself up as a heartless leader among heartless bandits. He was loyal to those who served him in every respect except one: he had no problem sacrificing them to save his own reputation. Thus, his minions would do his dirty work and be handsomely rewarded for their trouble, while Davies grew rich and powerful without being implicated in the capers he planned.

Both Hawkins and I testified against Davies and told what we had observed while a part of his gang. It seemed the case was pretty clear-cut, and I was sure it would be favorable for us. The jury retired to make their decision, and I waited in suspense until they returned and the judge pronounced the sentence. To our surprise, Davies did not receive capital punishment for his crimes. Instead, the judge ruled that Davies should serve the remainder of his life in a penal colony in the Andaman Islands.

A murmur arose in the courtroom. When I looked at Hawkins, he was already limping out the door. I hurried after him.

"Damn!" He spat when I caught up to him.

"It's not so bad. At least we won't have to deal with him for a long time."

"Forgive me," he said, resuming his normal tone, "but I had hoped his sentence would be slightly harsher."

"Well maybe it is better this way. The circle of revenge has to break some time."

He smiled. "Quite so."

HAWKINS DIDN'T WANT to go home, so we spent the rest of the day traveling around London, but he refused to speak. I noticed that he seemed a little closer to his normal self, and yet there was something that hinted otherwise. Big Ben struck four as we passed it, and Hawkins pulled out his pocket watch.

"I believe a sufficient amount of time has passed."

"For what?"

"Collins, I have someone I wish to visit. Would you care to join me?"

"Yeah, sure."

"Excellent!"

"So where are we going?"

"The prison."

The prison—Milbank Prison to be precise—wasn't too much of a drive from Westminster Abbey and we soon made it to Pimlico. The prison building was shaped like a flower, but its odd shape did little to dispel the imposing nature that hung like a fog around it. There were no smiles in that place, and I doubt that even Mr. Blessington with all his cheerfulness could have retained his buoyant air.

Hawkins had little trouble getting in once he gave his name to the constable at the gate. We were led through the jaws of that dark building to the main office. Hawkins spoke to the man in charge for a few moments, and we were relieved of any weapons before the Inspector showed us to a cell.

"You've an odd sense of timing, Mr. 'awkins," the man said. "We just got 'im settled in an hour or two ago. I don't think 'e'll be any too keen on visitors, but since you insist." He unlocked the door. We entered a small cell that contained a lonely looking man. The Inspector shut the door behind us with a loud bang, and Davies looked up from the ledge where he was sitting.

"You two!" he said harshly. "What the devil do you want? I have no desire to see you."

Hawkins sat down on the ledge near Davies and laid his cane across his knees. I stood near the door, feeling strangely claustrophobic but ready for anything.

"I merely wished to see how you were getting along, Bartholomew," Hawkins said in a genial tone.

"That is not my name; I gave it up long ago. If I must entertain you in my new lodgings, I insist you refer to me as Stephen."

"I apologize."

"Damn you, Jeremy. You've always been the better of me, and this is your crowning achievement isn't it? Well, go ahead and gloat then. That is what you came here to do, correct? Father did say I would end up in a jail cell one day."

"I did not come here to brag, Stephen; I came here to make amends."

"Amends? You put me in jail, and now you expect me to welcome you with open arms? I suppose next you'll want us to become friends."

"No, I don't expect us to be friends. I just want us to no longer be enemies."

"It's far too late for that. You are my greatest enemy, and I will have my revenge."

"Stephen, please, think of our father. He always wanted us to get along—"

"Our father? He was my father, and you stole him from me! The day you entered my life is a cursed day in history. Mark my words, Jeremy; I will have my revenge on you. You will curse the day you were born, and I will crush you as one crushes a beetle. It is my mission." He then turned away from us, and Hawkins sighed.

We left the prison and the brooding man who sat behind its walls. Hawkins limped along swiftly until we were free from its shadow and paused for a moment to put his gloves on. "So be it. I tried." He said simply.

When we arrived home that evening, we learned we had a visitor.

"Aggie!" I said with unrestrained joy as soon as I laid eyes on her. She smiled and rose from her seat on the couch. We embraced warmly, and she then greeted her brother. Mrs. Montgomery rose from where she had been sitting opposite Agatha and left the three of us alone together.

Agatha exclaimed, "Good evening, gentlemen! Your dear landlady wrote me in Paris to say that you had been having a few adventures, and now I see that she was quite right." She paused, gently fingering around my bruises. "Are you both quite well?"

"Yeah, we're pretty good for the most part," I replied. Hawkins limped past me and sat down in his armchair. Agatha and I sat down on the couch.

"Livesey, Mrs. Montgomery told me that there was a trial and a criminal gang involved. Was it Bartholomew?" she asked softly.

"Yes, I'm afraid it was. But he prefers to be known as Stephen these days."

She looked down sadly for a moment. "It is a pity. I had hoped that he might change some day."

"So, what brings you to our humble home?" I asked, trying to change the subject.

"Well, for Christmas, of course! I thought I might spend the holiday with you."

"That's an awesome idea!"

"I thought you might say that," she giggled. "By the way, Livesey, I am glad to see that you like your wreath."

She gestured toward the door where the wreath still hung upon Hawkins' knife, and I smiled at the memory of that day.

"It is a lovely wreath, I suppose," he said absentmindedly. He seemed to be in no mood for conversation, and excused himself from the room a few moments later. Once he had closed his bedroom door, Agatha turned to me and spoke in a low whisper. "Is he alright? He doesn't look well."

"He's been acting like that ever since we returned from the gang. Stephen forced him to kill someone."

"So that's it then. Well, perhaps if we just give him some time he'll come around."

"I hope you're right."

Mrs. Montgomery prepared the spare bedroom upstairs for Agatha's stay. After Christmas, she would return to Farnham, and I proposed that we return with her for the new year. She agreed readily to this, and Hawkins admitted that a few weeks in the country would do us both some good. For his sake, I hoped he was right.

I SPENT THE NEXT FEW DAYS completely immersed in Christmas spirit. London, a majestic sight despite some of its gruesome aspects, was beaming at Christmas. I felt like a character in Dickens' *A Christmas Carol*, which thrilled me to no end since that is one of my favorite books. Everyone seemed to be at his cheerful best, carols were sung, and there was even a little bit of snow with the promise of a white Christmas. Agatha and I went shopping a few times or just walked down the street holding hands. Christmas truly is the most wonderful time of the year.

We learned later that almost every member of the gang had been sentenced to hang, which was hardly surprising considering that they all had criminal records. The younger members of the gang, who had a chance for rehabilitation, were merely sentenced to prison time. They would be spending Christmas behind bars, but I had little pity for them. It was the lifestyle they had chosen.

On Christmas Eve, Thomas Blessington dropped by Montague Street and invited us gentlemen to join him for a drink. Hawkins declined since his leg was hurting him, but I thought it sounded like an excellent idea and opted to go. I promised Agatha I wouldn't be back too late and then accompanied Blessington to a friendly little pub with a cozy atmosphere and excellent ale.

I woke up the next morning on the couch in our sitting room still fully dressed and couldn't remember how I had ended up there. Not being much of a drinker. I remembered having only two drinks, but the hangover indicated it may have been more. My head throbbed, my stomach churned, and my tongue felt like I had licked a cotton ball. The ticking of the clock on the mantelpiece was almost unbearable, and I wished someone would make it stop.

"Good morning, my dear fellow, and a happy Christmas to you." I looked over at Hawkins, who was sitting in his chair with a weary expression on his face.

"What's so good about it?" I moaned.

"I haven't the slightest idea."

"How did I get here? And what did they put in that beer?"

"Blessington brought you home around eleven o'clock last night. He said that you had only had three drinks before you just passed out at the bar."

"Only three? Well that's embarrassing. Hey, do me a favor, remind me never to drink again."

"Certainly."

I received little sympathy from my still brooding friend and even less from Mrs. Montgomery. She didn't approve of drunkenness, and she made that fact clear. Agatha was more amused by my Christmas Eve adventure. However, I saw nothing amusing in it, and I made a mental note to imbibe more carefully in the future.

As the day progressed I recovered from the hangover and partook in the Christmas festivities cheerfully. Blessington visited in the afternoon to see how I was doing and to wish all "the season's greetings." It seemed as though he had no one to spend Christmas with, so we invited had him to share the festivities with us. His cheerful attitude lent more happiness to our meager celebration.

Later in the evening, it started snowing, and we dimmed the lights in the sitting room so we could watch the snow. Hawkins opened a window slightly, and we heard Christmas carolers singing "Silent Night." Mrs. Montgomery entered, carrying a tray with five glasses and a bottle of champagne.

"Champagne, Mrs. Montgomery?" I asked.

"Yes, doctor, I thought we might have a toast or two to celebrate the season."

"What a splendid idea!" Agatha said with a smile. I felt my stomach churn at the thought of more alcohol.

"If you don't mind, I think I will stick to water," I said.

"A wise decision," Mrs. Montgomery said somewhat coldly as she poured the fermented liquid. We lifted our glasses—mine was filled with water, I assure you—while Mrs. Montgomery proposed a toast.

"To family," she said simply. We each echoed her and clinked our glasses gently. To family indeed! My family was not only thousands of miles away but in another time period. However, I had never felt like I belonged as much as I felt I belonged in the presence of these four unique people. As I sipped my water, I realized that they had become my family. This was where I belonged, and my home was here in the 19th century—and not the 21st. After an entire life in the future, I had discovered that my present was in the past, and I was content for the first time in my life. Outside, the carolers were reaching the end of their song, and the words couldn't have been more fitting.

Sleep in heavenly peace, sleep in heavenly peace.

✳ CHAPTER XII

THE DAY AFTER CHRISTMAS, HAWKINS AND
I left with Agatha for Surrey. We prepared for New Year's
Eve, which I learned was a grand tradition at Townsend Grange.
On December 31, a drove of Agatha's neighbors and friends
appeared at the Grange. There was a feast, some dancing, and
fireworks at midnight. I recognized some of the people from my
last visit but most were unfamiliar to me. I discovered that my
hated rival, Lord Roberts, had been able to win over Miss Francis
Higgins. In fact, they were engaged, and I wished them well, even
though Roberts still sneered at me whenever our eyes met.

Hawkins seemed to disappear as soon as we arrived at
Townsend Grange. We caught glimpses of him here and there, but
he kept entirely to himself, and Agatha told me to just let him be.
She did ask her butler to keep her apprised of Hawkins' movements,
and he would give us a report each morning at breakfast. One
morning, we were informed that "Mr. Hawkins was seen walking
toward Aula Creek," while another time he was "found asleep in
the branches of the oak tree next to the stables," and once we were
told that he had been seen in a pasture mingling with the bovines.
As his friend, I was worried about him, but this was something he
had to work out himself.

After New Year's Day, things settled down. We received plenty of snow, and Agatha and I often went out for sleigh rides. There was a large pond near the house that froze completely to the bottom. Agatha had never skated on it before, but since I loved to ice skate, I taught her how. The ice skates of the century were different than what I was used to, mainly because they strapped to the bottom of one's shoes, but it didn't take me long to get the knack.

Winter at Townsend Grange was like living in a storybook. It was a wonderful feeling to just play, and Agatha and I behaved like children. We built an army of snowmen on the front lawns, sledded down hills, and often returned to the house soaking wet and laughing. There were several snowball fights, which often grew to involve the entire staff, ending with cups of hot cocoa for all. We were occasionally forced to spend days indoors and would play all sorts of card games. Once we even played hide and go seek in the vast house. I believe Agatha won most of the games. She was such a wonderfully alive person, and 1893 was by far the best winter of my life.

All good things must come to an end, and the fun of winter melted into the beauty of spring. Sunny and rainy days vied for supremacy, and all were special in their own way. At Townsend Grange, there was a wonderful smell that accompanied each season. In the summer, the smell was warm, which I associated with fresh-cut hay. The autumn smell was colder than summer, but with a peculiar spiciness added. Winter smelled plainly cold and wet, but the spring smelled alive. The English countryside had a quality of air that would no doubt disappear as the years went by and pollution became global, but I felt fortunate to be able to enjoy so much of it. The air was like a tonic, for everything seemed to be robust and strong. Even the people who had lived their lives in the country seemed healthier than most of the people in London, but this didn't really surprise me due to the toxic air in that city.

Agatha and I mellowed from our youthful winter pastimes into more adult spring-time actions, but sometimes relapsed into the childishness. One day, Agatha asked me if I would help her weed one of the flower beds, and we ended up throwing weeds and dirt at each other while laughing hysterically. It took us awhile to clean up our mess, but we did get the flower bed weeded eventually. When we weren't attempting to garden, we went horseback riding across the green fields of Townsend Grange. There were plenty of other activities besides. Thus the spring days went blissfully by and were filled with the smell of life, the sound of birds, and the sight of Agatha's beautiful smile.

ONE FINE MORNING in the middle of April as Agatha and I sat down to breakfast, we were surprised by the arrival of Hawkins. He limped to the table, sat down, and began eating as soon as the maid fetched him a plate. He looked a bit thinner than the last time I had seen him, and he seemed tired somehow, but with a certain peace about him. Agatha and I exchanged a look. Hawkins looked up from his plate and studied our faces.

"Good morning," he offered.

"Good morning to you as well," Agatha said with a smile.

"We've missed you these past few months," I said.

"It has been an interesting time, but not completely wasted I suspect. I trust that the two of you have been well?"

"Well, I fell off of Royal when we were riding yesterday and sprained my ankle slightly, but other than that I'd say it's been pretty fun." Royal was one of Agatha's many beautiful horses, and he had rapidly become my favorite.

"Livesey," Agatha said in a low voice while looking him straight in the eyes, "are you quite well?" He paused and smiled in return. The fire had returned to his eyes, and the turmoil that had been there was completely gone.

"Yes, Aggie, I am."

AFTER THAT, THE THREE of us went on much the same as we had the last time Hawkins and I had visited, but with one notable exception. There was no music in the house. I had told Agatha the sad fate of her brother's unfortunate violin, and she decided it would be best if we avoided the subject of music for awhile.

One day, the weather was so inclement that the three of us were driven into the parlor by its harshness. I watched as the rain pounded the earth violently and the wind blew threw the trees like the breath of a musician through his instrument. The symphony they played was unlike any other, and I wondered if this strange orchestra could withstand its own melody.

Hawkins and Agatha resumed their chess game, and I alternated between watching them, perusing a book, and observing the performance of the windy weather through the window. I was observing that it was really more of a ballet than a symphony when all of a sudden an exclamation of surprise came from the chess game.

"Ha! Checkmate!" Hawkins declared triumphantly.

"What?" Agatha asked incredulously, studying the chessboard with disbelief.

"No way!" I said.

Hawkins sat back in his chair and folded his arms across his chest smugly. Agatha started laughing and congratulated him heartily. "I thought this game would never end!" she laughed.

"So you see, after all, I was correct when I said that you could not beat me."

"Oh, it was only because I wasn't paying attention that you beat me in the first place."

"Shall we try again and settle this once and for all?"

"Absolutely not!"

"Wait, so how many moves did that take?" I asked.

"That is an excellent question, but I have no idea," Hawkins replied.

Before Hawkins could celebrate his victory, the butler entered with a letter.

"Pardon the interruption gentlemen, my lady," he said in his dignified butler manner, "but a letter has arrived for Mr. Hawkins."

"Thank you, my good sir," Hawkins said as he took the letter. He read the contents and sighed. "It seems there is a distressed duke in London, and he is requesting my advice."

"A duke? Wow! That's pretty high up there," I said.

"Indeed. I helped a friend of his once, it seems, although the name isn't entirely familiar to me. Anyway, I must return to London immediately."

"Oh." I said.

"You do not by any means have to accompany me, my dear fellow."

"Yeah, but I think I should anyway. I've been neglecting Mrs. Montgomery all this time."

"Well, I shall miss the pair of you. I promise I will come down to London and visit you soon." Agatha said.

And so we left the beautiful fairy-tale countryside with its healing air behind and returned to the labyrinth of London.

I CANNOT DESCRIBE how incredibly dull the city seemed after five months in the English countryside. I was rather depressed when we stepped off the train. Hawkins, by contrast, was in a dapper mood, his eyes gleaming as he surveyed his surroundings. His leg had healed well during our stay in the country, and although he kept the cane with him, he didn't rely on it so much. He still had a pronounced limp, and I knew he wouldn't be as active as he once was.

Because we had taken the late train, it was evening when we arrived in London and dark when we reached good old 37c Montague Street. Mrs. Montgomery was still up when we arrived and greeted us warmly. Hawkins asked her if she would bring up some food for us since we had not dined. She went off to do so with a smile on her face.

The sitting room was uncharacteristically tidy but otherwise unchanged as we entered it. A cheerful fire crackled in the fireplace, and the clock on the mantelpiece still boldly kept time as it always had. The wreath was gone from the door—a slit in the woodwork testified that it had once hung there. Hawkins pulled his pipe out of his pocket and chewed on it as he stood in front of the fireplace with one arm behind his back, studying the portrait hanging above the mantelpiece. It was then that I noticed the intact violin sitting in his chair.

"Hawkins, look!" I said, indicating the repaired instrument. He whirled around and slowly walked to the chair with a look of astonishment on his face. He carefully picked up his beloved instrument and held it with a look of loving fondness for a moment.

"Ah, Mrs. Montgomery," he said quietly with a smile. The bow was also lying in the chair, and he picked it up and drew it carefully across the strings with a sigh of satisfaction, even though it was dreadfully out of tune. He quickly tuned it. I sat down on the couch to listen while Hawkins played for the first time in several months. Mrs. Montgomery entered silently with the dinner tray and joined me on the couch to also listen.

He played for quite some time—silhouetted by the fire behind him with his eyes tightly shut. I had never in my life heard such beautiful music. When he finished, Mrs. Montgomery and I paused as the final vestiges of the notes faded into the silence. We applauded him heartily, and Hawkins dropped wearily into his chair with a smile.

"Thank you." he said, inclining his head graciously.

"It's good to have the two of you home. I missed you terribly," said Mrs. Montgomery with a motherly sort of affection. She rose and headed for the door but paused before exiting to say, "Goodnight, sirs."

"It is good to be back, Mrs. Montgomery," said Hawkins. "Goodnight to you as well." I echoed this sentiment, and she left us alone in the sitting room.

We ate our dinner and then sat and talked until the clock chimed midnight.

"Well, old chap," Hawkins said as he stood up and stretched, "it is rather late isn't it? Goodnight."

"Goodnight, Hawkins" I replied. He disappeared into his room, and I was left alone. I remained on the couch, letting my mind wander where it would. Hawkins had left his violin sitting in his chair, and for the first time I noticed what an odd instrument it was. Unlike most violins that were a reddish color, Hawkins' was a very dark mahogany. I walked to it and carefully picked it up to examine it better.

Remarkably, it hadn't been terribly damaged when it fell down the stairs, and I could just barely make out a few places where some cosmetic damage had been fixed. There were carvings along the edge of the violin that were more decorative than what most instruments are adorned with. Hawkins explained he had found the instrument in a pawn shop, which was unusual in itself because he didn't generally visit such establishments. However, the instrument had drawn his attention because of its unique qualities, and he had bought it from the pawn broker for 10 shillings. He then attempted to discover its origins but was never successful, and the instrument's history remained a mystery.

I carefully replaced the instrument on Hawkins' chair and mused on how well it suited its singular owner. They were both unique in their own ways—and both had abstruse pasts. Neither had been claimed by their original owners, but they made a good life with their rescuers. What would life be like if events like these were completely random? What if there was nothing controlling the universe, and we just galloped along like a rider less horse? There are people who believe that such events occur as they will, but I believe this is impossible. If life was totally random, the earth would have ceased to exist long ago.

❉ CHAPTER XIII

MAY RACED INTO JUNE, AND JUNE sauntered along with a show of hot, humid weather. The days went by agonizingly slow for me, although Hawkins was kept rather busy—thanks to the duke he had advised upon our return. He was usually out of the house before I woke up and returned late at night exhausted. Therefore, I had time to think and ponder in his absence. My thoughts dwelled consistently on Agatha, and I decided that I wanted to marry her.

While it's true that there were many objections to Agatha and me becoming a couple—mainly that I had no means of supporting her and that we had only known one another for less than a year—I loved her more than I had loved anyone else, and I knew that she felt the same. Many people don't believe in love at first sight, but Agatha and I are proof that it does happen.

Since Agatha didn't have a father, I felt it was my duty to approach Hawkins and ask him permission to marry his sister. After all, he was her elder by all of five years. Because I saw so little of him, I had plenty of time to think of what I was going to say and how I was going to say it. However, when I walked into the sitting room one Saturday morning with the intention of discussing the matter with him and found Hawkins sitting at the table sipping his tea and reading The London Times, my mind went blank.

"Good morning, Collins," he said. I was always a bit tentative when it came to Hawkins' moods first thing in the morning, but he seemed to be in a cheerful mood at the time.

"Oh, uh, good morning" I said, still surprised at his presence. "I didn't think I'd see you today."

"Ah, yes, I have been rather absent lately haven't I? It was not in vain I assure you. The matter was perfectly childish, but it required a lot of research at the outset. Now it is up to my distressed client to do what he can with the advice I have given him. I must admit, I have little confidence that he will carry out my instructions."

He seemed to be waiting for me to make some remark in response, but my attention was riveted on the tea pot, so I hadn't paid much attention to what he had said.

"Collins? I say, Collins are you alright?" he asked, somewhat concerned. I stirred at his question.

"Oh, yeah, I'm ok. Hawkins, there's something I want to ask you. It's, well, um, it's kind of important." I paused to gather my thoughts, but found to my horror that I had none on hand.

"Well, what is it man?"

The impatience in Hawkins' voice did nothing to calm my nerves, and I ended up blurting out some unintelligible nonsense. He looked at me questioningly for a moment, before breaking out into a wide smile.

"Now then, Collins, I'm afraid I don't speak gibberish, so would you please reiterate, slowly and carefully."

I took a deep breath, kicking myself for looking like a fool. "I want to marry your sister," I said slowly. Hawkins smiled and jumped to his feet.

"Excellent! I was wondering if you were ever going to do it!" He shook my hand and slapped me on the back. I looked at him with a dazed expression. It had all been far too easy.

"Wait, that's it? You're not going to argue or chastise me or anything like that?" I asked tentatively.

"My dear doctor, how could you think such a thing? I would

never do that to you!"

"Hmm, well I'm not so sure about that."

Hawkins burst out into a hearty laugh and I couldn't help but join. We were interrupted in our merriment by a soft knock on the door.

"What in heaven's name is going on up here?" asked Mrs. Montgomery as she entered carrying the mail.

"Only that we are soon to have a wedding, dear Mrs. Montgomery!" said Hawkins. "Collins is going to ask for Agatha's hand!"

"Oh my! This is wonderful news indeed! Congratulations, sir!" Mrs. Montgomery shook my hand, gave Hawkins the mail, and then retreated from our joyful presence.

"So do you think she'll say yes?" I asked as I plopped down in an armchair, still feeling overjoyed but a little breathless.

"Absolutely!" he said, as he opened a letter. "She's sure to be pleased." His voice trailed off and his brow furrowed as he read the letter.

"What is it, Hawkins?" I asked. He started and forced a smile.

"Oh, it's nothing, nothing at all." He walked over to the fire and threw the letter into it. I wouldn't have thought much of it, but the fact that he didn't even attempt to explain the letter aroused my suspicions. My instinct told me to act. I dashed to the fire and retrieved the letter before it was consumed.

"Hawkins, this is a death threat!" I said incredulously after I had read its short contents.

"Not exactly. It is a precursor to a death threat. I've been expecting something like this."

"Who do you think it's from?"

"No doubt a member of the gang who escaped custody."

"So, shouldn't we involve the police or something?" I asked.

"No, it is not worth it."

"Are you sure? I really think—"

"My dear Collins, this is why I was loath to let you view the letter in the first place. You make much of a trifle. Besides, you must prepare for your imminent betrothal."

"But I—"

"Now, none of that Collins, it does you no credit. Let's see, ah yes! I have the perfect strategy for you." He paced the room as he spoke, talking to himself more than to me and allowing me no opportunity to speak. "I will wire Agatha and have her here this evening. Then, you will meet her as she alights from the train, and you can proposition her on the way to her hotel. Yes, she must stay at the hotel. It would be highly inappropriate for her to stay here. Of course, we will have to leave immediately to book her a room at the Langham. Oh, it is perfect! Now, what do you say to that, dear doctor?"

"Uhhh—"

"Splendid! We must be off immediately, for there is much to do and little time to do it. Come, come, Collins! Don't dawdle." He was already in the hall, and I felt as though I had just witnessed a tornado whirling around the room. However, I managed to gather my wits about me and hurried after him as quickly as I could.

Hawkins and I spent the rest of the day in a flurry of activity. He helped me choose and pay for an engagement ring, planned my evening, decided that the weather would hold long enough for me to walk Agatha the last two blocks to her hotel, made a few suggestions, and finally sent me off on my errand. Somewhere in the midst of all this, he sent Agatha an urgent telegram asking her to come to London immediately, and she wired back saying she would catch the first train she could. This put her arrival somewhere around eight that evening, and I would be the one to pick her up.

I couldn't help but feel like this was all a bit rushed, and I was nervous by the time I was supposed to leave.

"All right, Dr. Collins, there you are," Mrs. Montgomery said as she helped me into my coat.

"Thanks, Mrs. Montgomery. I'm sure it'll be ok. I mean, she's bound to say yes, right? Well, either way we'll be back kind of late," I said, shaking from head to foot in my excitement.

"Yes sir, you already said that."

"I did?"

"Twice in fact." She smiled that motherly smile of hers, and I couldn't help but laugh.

"Oh, well, I guess I did. Goodbye, Mrs. Montgomery, I'll see you later."

"Goodbye, sir, and good luck!"

"Thanks, I'm sure I'll need it. A lot of it." I climbed into the cab with a knot in my stomach, and Mrs. Montgomery waved at me from the bottom step of the house before disappearing inside. I looked up to the second-story window and saw Hawkins standing there smiling and chewing on his pipe. I steeled myself for the task ahead and told the cabby to drive on.

The trip to Waterloo Station seemed far too short, but I managed to calm myself down quite a bit before we arrived. My legs still shook a little as I climbed out of the cab, but my voice sounded perfectly calm as I asked him to wait.

Her train hadn't arrived yet, so I stood on the platform rehearsing my plans and fingering the ring in my pocket. It was a beauty of a ring, although simple. It was merely a band of silver, but apparently such things were the custom of the era. At any rate, Agatha preferred simplicity when it came to jewelry. She believed that an object's beauty was deeper than the surface indicated, and she enjoyed looking deeper. I once saw her studying the complexity of a pebble with childlike wonder. She would have been a great artist.

I was interrupted in my musings by the arrival of Agatha's train. It entered the station with a rush of wind and a cloud of steam before screeching to a halt. A flood of humanity poured from it. I searched through the crowd until I finally picked her out.

"Agatha!" I shouted as I made my way through the mass. She heard me over the din and turned toward me with a smile.

"Why, Andrew! I didn't expect you to be here to get me!" We embraced and then kissed for a moment before she pulled away from me in alarm. "What's the emergency? What's happened?"

"Huh? What emergency?" I asked.

"Livesey said in his telegram that there was an emergency, but he did not say what it was."

"Oh, right! I'd forgotten about that. Well, there's not actually an emergency. Kind of." I felt sheepish, and she put her arms akimbo while fixing a stern look on me.

"You mean to say that I rushed all the way out here for nothing? This is intolerable! I will not be summoned up for trifling reasons, and you may tell my dear brother that I am returning home this instant!" She turned to leave, and I hoped to salvage the situation. This was not at all how I had pictured the evening.

"Aggie, wait!" I took her hand, and she stopped abruptly.

"What is it?" She said crossly.

The people around us were staring curiously, and I felt like I had an audience. I ignored them, however, and dropped down on one knee, still holding her hand. She stared at me curiously, for it was not customary for Victorians to kneel when proposing.

"I want to tell you something—something very important. This isn't the way I had imagined it, but I guess it will have to work." I paused and took a deep breath before continuing. "Agatha, I love you. From the moment I first saw you standing in front of that grand house of yours, I loved you, and because of this love I want to spend the rest of my life with you. Agatha, would you do me the honor of becoming my bride?"

I timed it just so I could pull the ring out of my pocket at the culmination of my speech, and she stood breathless for a moment before giving me her response.

"Oh, Andrew! Yes! Absolutely! A million times yes!" She cried, and I slipped the ring on her finger while a chorus of ahs went up from the crowd. I stood up, and we kissed again. So the best-laid plans for a romantic evening were compromised; yet, I left Waterloo Station hand-in-hand with my fiancée. I often felt that it would've been less wonderful if everything had worked out according to Hawkins' plan, and I believe that he knew Agatha would react strongly to being summoned for no reason. He, of course, refused to tell me for certain, but I suppose it doesn't matter. He is after all a master strategist.

Agatha and I spent the rest of the evening together—walking, holding hands, and talking about how weddings and engagements were done in the current era. I learned of a few social blunders I had made, but she assured me that none of them made the slightest difference to her. By the time I saw her safely to her hotel, I was perfectly happy that I thought I should die from being overjoyed. I skipped down the street—in the wrong direction no less—feeling like I might explode if I didn't release some of my joy.

It was late before I finally returned to Montague Street. Mrs. Montgomery had long since retired, and there was no sign that Hawkins was stirring either. I was still in a state of bliss, but skipping down the street had brought me back down to earth. I didn't realize how very worn out I was until I lay down and fell immediately into a deep sleep.

✳ CHAPTER XIV

URING MY STAY IN LONDON, I WAS periodically overwhelmed by my situation, but I always found comfort in confiding in my friend, Livesey Hawkins. He listened to my rants with the greatest care and attention and then offered some piece of reasoning that calmed me. Never did I need his collected intellect more than on the morning following my engagement to Agatha. I awoke with the terror that comes from a hasty decision and immediately went to Hawkins to vent my fears.

"I can't believe that I did this! What the holy heck was I thinking? No wait, I wasn't using my freaking brain at all; I just rushed into it! Gosh, I'm such an idiot!" I paced the room, waving my arms as I berated myself. "I mean, how am I supposed to support her? I don't even have a job, for Pete's sake! She doesn't deserve me. She needs a good, decent gentleman, not an impulsive guy from the wrong century."

I dropped onto the couch after I finished my tirade and waited for Hawkins to say something comforting. When he said nothing, I looked up and was astonished to find him glowering at me.

"What? Why are you looking at me like that?" I asked.

"Because you are behaving like a thorough and unmitigated ass."

I was taken completely aback by his austerity, and was at a loss for words. "But I—"

"Oh, please, just stop this instant! You are feeling sorry for yourself and being entirely selfish."

"Selfish? How am I being selfish?"

"You have completely neglected to consider Agatha's feelings."

I realized that he was absolutely correct. I had been so captivated with my own fears that I hadn't considered what Agatha might feel. "Oh."

"Quite so. Now, let us put things into perspective." He shifted in his chair and addressed me as he might a classroom of students. "Fact number one: You did not rush into this decision. You never rush into anything, which is why I forced you to propose to Agatha last night. I knew you would wait otherwise. Fact number two: I have little doubt that you will have no need for an occupation unless it is to alleviate your boredom, and I doubt you will have much of that. The estate receives a handsome income—which I know you will not abuse—therefore Agatha does not need to be supported. Fact number three: Whether Agatha deserves you or not is quite beside the question."

"What do you mean?"

"It is simple. Do you love her?"

"Yes, of course!"

"I know for a fact that she reciprocates, and that is all that matters, is it not?"

"Well, I guess so."

"There is no guessing here, my dear Doctor. In my experience—and it is considerable—I have found that where there is genuine love, there is a way."

"Oh, it's like that one Beetle's song, 'All You Need is Love.'"

"What?"

"Never mind."

"Well, I do not want to hear of you doubting this relationship ever again, do you understand?"

"Ok, ok!"

"And Agatha isn't to know about it either."

"Fine."

"Excellent."

After that conversation, I never again questioned the wisdom of my decision. This was partly because there was certain logic to what Hawkins said and partly because the look he had given me impressed me as unfavorable.

There was much ado over the details of our wedding. Agatha wanted to have it as soon as possible, I wanted to wait a few months, and Hawkins didn't care. We finally decided on November 9—a Wednesday. We both agreed to a small ceremony. Hawkins, Mrs. Montgomery, and Mr. Blessington would be the only people invited. It was possible that random passersby would drop in also, since it was against the law to marry behind closed doors.

Overall, the whole prospect of so simple a wedding appealed to me greatly. Marriage wasn't nearly so big a deal to the Victorians, but I had always dreaded that there would be much pomp at my wedding. My only regret was that my brother would not be there to see me marry. However, I was to be wed among the closest friends I had ever had.

After the wedding, Agatha and I would spend a week or two in France as our honeymoon and then return to Townsend Hall. The rest of my life would be spent as a country squire, with my beautiful wife supporting me every step of the way. It certainly wasn't a bad fate, and I knew I would be happy.

My life was so full of happiness, that I couldn't believe it was possible. I would wake every day and pinch myself to make sure I wasn't dreaming because it seemed so surreal. The days seemed to pass slowly and yet fly by. I could hardly wait to be married, but being with Agatha every day was so memorable that I cherished every moment until we parted for the evening. What a wonderful sort of ambivalence love creates! You are joyful because you love and are loved, but sorrowful because you know it may end someday.

NOVEMBER 9 WAS A RAINY DAY. I arose early in the morning, my stomach one big knot of anxiety, and wasn't quite sure what to do with myself. I went down to the sitting room and watched the rain fall in the darkness. The clock chimed six a.m., a log crackled in the fireplace, and the rain beat a steady rhythm on the pavement below.

"Dismal weather is this. However, I am sure it will clear up before long."

I jumped nearly out of my skin and spun around to face Hawkins. He was fully dressed and bore the signs of a man who has not slept all night. "Hawkins, you scared me."

"I am terribly sorry, old boy, but I assure you that it was not my intention." He hobbled over to my chair next to the fireplace, favoring his leg more than usual.

"You know, you really need to have your leg looked at by a doctor again."

"Collins, we have had this discussion before."

"And we're going to have it again unless you do what you're told."

"Humph, well we can discuss it later. It is your wedding day, and I think you will want to be on good terms with your brother-in-law."

"Yeah, I suppose so."

We sat in silence with only the dying fire to light the room. I gradually watched the world outside grow lighter, and Hawkins watched the fireplace as it fell into darkness. We were both aroused from our separate reveries when the clock chimed seven. Mrs. Montgomery came bustling into the room soon after to relight the fire and was obviously startled to find us both up and about. She had sense enough to remain silent and left the room quietly after rebuilding the fire.

A half hour elapsed before we were interrupted again. Mrs. Montgomery entered quietly with a pot of hot, steaming tea and biscuits for the two of us. This would have to suffice until after the wedding when we would return for breakfast.

"I can't believe I'm getting married," I said, partially to myself and partially to Hawkins and Mrs. Montgomery. Neither one of them answered me.

THERE WERE NO wedding bells that day. No organ bellowed the traditional wedding march. No bishop united Agatha and me in holy matrimony. Yet, there was no wedding which could have been finer in my opinion. Mrs. Montgomery left the house before Hawkins and me so she could be with Agatha, and it seemed safer to let the ladies do their womanly thing unhindered by any men. Thomas Blessington, with a smile so broad it seemed like his round face would split, arrived not long after and we had a final drink to toast the end of my bachelor days. We then left for the small church where the ceremony was to be held.

Mrs. Montgomery and Agatha had not yet arrived by the time we did, and I nervously paced in front of the altar while we waited. Hawkins and Blessington talked to the pastor, who was a young man with a cheerful face. A couple of random people came and went in the interval—all of them staring curiously and wondering what was going on.

All of a sudden, Hawkins took out his violin, which he had brought with him, and started playing Jesu, Joy of Man's Desiring. When I turned around, I saw Agatha walking down the isle of the church with Mrs. Montgomery, and my nerves immediately calmed down. She wasn't wearing an extravagant wedding dress; it was simply her best dress with a veil. She never looked lovelier. The ceremony proceeded without further ado, and it seemed an eternity before the pastor finally said, "You may now kiss the bride." Thus, in one passionate kiss, my bachelor days ended, and my life was forever different.

Mrs. Montgomery openly cried when the ceremony ended, and Hawkins comforted her with a smile on his face. The five of us thanked the pastor and left the church to head back to Montague Street for breakfast and a celebration. Mrs. Montgomery had prepared most of the breakfast before she left that morning, but she still had a lot to do in order to finish it. Agatha insisted on helping her, so the three of us men were left alone in the sitting room with our brandy glasses.

"Ha ha ha! By Jove, Collins, you're a married man. You'll have to watch yourself now!" Mr. Blessington exclaimed with a laugh as I poured myself a half glass of brandy.

"You guys just wait until you're married. I'll be able to brag about how much better my wife is than yours!" I laughed heartily, and Blessington readily joined in. Hawkins, by contrast, sat silently with his fingertips pressed together and brows knit.

"Well, sir, I don't reckon Hawkins 'ere will ever take a wife; there's none as could stand him!" Blessington said with a conspiratorial wink at me. Hawkins stirred at the sound of his name and looked up with a smile.

"I'm terribly sorry, gentlemen, what were you saying?"

Mr. Blessington and I exchanged a glance and then busted into an uncontrollable fit of laughter. Hawkins smiled, but his eyes shot daggers. I was so very cheerful, that not even his harsh looks could silence me. Blessington lit a cigarette and blew a cloud of smoke into the air.

Blessington continued, "We were just discussing future wives. See now, I've had my eye on this pretty young woman who lives on my street. She's a fine lady, and I reckon one of these days I'll propose to her when I've saved up enough to support her."

"How interesting," Hawkins said blandly.

I shot him a look of reproach and then gave Blessington my best smile. "Really? I need to meet her someday!" I said with enthusiasm.

"Oh, she's a dazzling woman! Anyway, my point is, I've got a gal, but who does Mr. Hawkins have?" He looked at Hawkins genially, but the subject of his inquiry seemed downcast. It was the first time I had seen Hawkins at a loss for words. I cleared my throat and was about to change the subject when Agatha came in and announced that breakfast was ready. Hawkins sighed in relief and we went down to the dining room.

Mrs. Montgomery had turned the dining room into her private sitting room when she started leasing out the house, but it was also the only room with a table large enough for all of us. She had cleaned it and organized it so that it would have been fit for Queen Victoria herself.

The food was wonderful, and it was consumed readily by us half-starved wedding guests. Once we had all eaten our fill—and probably a little extra—I proposed that the men clean up in exchange for the wonderful food. Mrs. Montgomery protested that "it wasn't the proper thing to do," but Hawkins was in favor of my idea and easily convinced her. So the two women retired to the sitting room upstairs, and I coached Blessington and Hawkins in the subtle art of dishwashing.

An hour and three broken plates later, the three of us returned to the sitting room, soaked as we were, with the tea tray.

"Gentlemen, we were beginning to worry about you!" Agatha said with a giggle.

"It was quite a battle, but we eventually triumphed," Hawkins said as he poured tea for everyone.

"Battle. Yeah, that's definitely the word for it. You taught me well, Mrs. M., but I couldn't teach these two," I said.

"I think I did pretty well for a man who has never washed dishes before." Mr. Blessington replied indignantly.

"You were the worst of us!" Hawkins exclaimed.

"I hate to say it, but Hawkins is right, Thomas."

"I was really so terrible?" He looked so pitiful, but I nodded my affirmation.

"Ah well, I suppose my future does not lie in housekeeping," he said with a laugh.

And so the day advanced until everyone knew it was time to depart. Blessington was the first to leave. He shook my hand heartily, kissed Agatha on the cheek, wished us happiness, and then departed. The room was far quieter without his cheerful presence, and those of us who remained sat in silence.

"Andrew, dear, we need to be going if we are to catch our train," Agatha said quietly after a little while.

"Yeah." I sat for a little while longer and then stood up. I hated saying goodbye to anyone, but I couldn't put this off any longer. Agatha said goodbye to Hawkins while I loaded my suitcase onto the cab.

I walked back up the stairs to the sitting room one last time to gather my hat and say farewell to Hawkins. Those stairs seemed so different somehow. I had walked up them a hundred times over the past year, but they stood out so vividly this day. I had never noticed that the third stair from the top creaked, that the wallpaper on the wall had roses in its pattern, or even that the banister had a deep scratch running down its length. I paused at the door to the sitting room and studied the mark where Hawkins had hung the wreath with his knife. A little bit of daylight came through the slit, and it held me transfixed for just a moment before I pushed open the door and entered the room.

Hawkins was standing with his back to me, staring out the window, chewing on his pipe. He didn't turn around as I entered, and I debated what I was going to say to him. My throat felt tight, and I swallowed a few times in order to clear it.

"Well, um, I guess this is the last time we'll see each other for awhile."

"It may or may not be. None can tell the future and what will happen."

"Yeah. Hey, um, thank you. For everything I mean."

He turned around and faced me, but didn't look into my eyes.

"No, my dear fellow, thank you. For an entire year you have endured me, and I am grateful to have had the pleasure of your company." He held out his hand to me, which was kind of a big deal for him, and I shook it heartily. He then returned to the window and resumed chewing on his pipe. I gathered my coat and hat and left the room without another word. Sometimes silence is better than speech.

A tearful Mrs. Montgomery greeted me as I descended the stairs, and I couldn't help notice the contrast between her and Hawkins.

"There, there, Mrs. M.," I said as soothingly as I could. "There's no reason to cry."

"Oh, Mr. Collins, I shall miss you terribly!" she sobbed. I

couldn't bear to see her cry, so I pulled her to me so she wouldn't notice that I was weeping. Agatha stood nearby with a tearful smile. This was definitely harder on me than it was on her.

The sky had cleared as we climbed into the cab, but the clouds in the distance told us it wouldn't last long. I looked up at the house that I had lived in for a year, and I suddenly felt lonely without the presence of Hawkins who had been my ballast through many rough days. I felt adrift, but I steeled myself for the voyage ahead, waved goodbye to Mrs. Montgomery, and signaled the driver to drive off.

Agatha had left instructions before the wedding that her luggage should be sent from the hotel, so we went straight to the train station without stopping at the Langham.

"Andrew, are you all right?" Agatha asked in her gentle manner when I remained silent throughout the carriage ride.

"Yes, I'm just going to miss—that house is all." She smiled knowingly and squeezed my hand.

"I'm sure he'll miss you also."

I looked up at her and smiled. It was obvious that I wasn't going to be able to keep any secrets from her.

"Ah well. To France we go! And then you can teach me how to be a country squire. Ok?"

"It sounds like an excellent idea!"

THE TRAIN WAS RUNNING late, so when we arrived at the station we had to wait. The platform was unusually deserted for that time of day. All of a sudden, I felt the barrel of a gun pressed into my back, and a man's voice whispered to me to keep quiet and do as I was told. Another man slipped behind Agatha and told her the same thing, and I felt a shot of terror run up my spine. We were led away from the station into a dark alley, where we were blindfolded and bound. Our assailants shoved us into a carriage of some sort, and we were off almost before the door shut.

The carriage ride was fast-paced and lasted for what seemed like an eternity as we careened through the streets of London. I had no idea where we were, or where we were going, or even what time it was; my entire being was focused on Agatha and staying calm for her sake. When the carriage stopped, we were roughly forced out and onto what felt like a wooden pier. I could smell salt water in the air, and I heard the sound of water. It occurred to me that we were next to the Thames. We were forced onto a boat that took us across a river. Once out of the boat, we were taken into a building. Only then were our blindfolds taken off. The building was dim despite the sunlight that came through its solitary window, full of crates, and smelled musty. I thought the building seemed familiar, but I was too flustered to think. Agatha and I were forced to sit on two crates while our legs were bound. We were left alone in the darkness to await our fate.

✳ CHAPTER XV

AGATHA AND I WERE LEFT ALONE FOR some time. We tried to untie our hands and legs, but it was impossible, and we were compelled to give up. As the hours passed, I began to get the feeling that we might not make it out of this situation alive.

"Agatha?" I said softly. I felt her stir next to me.

"Yes, Andrew?" she replied.

"I just want you to know that I love you."

"Oh Andrew, I love you, too. We are going to make it out of this, I am sure."

Her voice was choked with tears, and she leaned her head on my chest. I felt somewhat cowardly, for I knew it was my job to comfort her and not the other way around.

"So, do you think they'll let us keep our reservation in Paris?" I tried to joke, but it didn't quite work.

"Perhaps we can go somewhere a little more local instead," she offered.

"I hear that Cornwall is freezing cold this time of year." This time, I managed to evoke a giggle from my wife.

"We could even go to America if you wished."

"Yeah, but the thing is, I've already seen America, and there's nothing there that is better than England."

So we talked about where to go on our honeymoon among other topics. Planning the future was somehow calming, and it took our minds off of our current situation.

Sometime in the night, she fell asleep with her head on my shoulder, and I soon followed her example. When I awoke, I could see the sun shining in through the window, and I further studied the building's gloomy interior.

It was a well-stocked warehouse littered with high stacks of all sorts of crates, and there was a balcony with a staircase that gave access to the upper offices. It was the same warehouse where Hawkins and I had been spies for three weeks. I saw a well-dressed man in a frock coat, black trousers, and spats leaning on the balcony reading a newspaper. His face was hidden from me by the paper, but there was something familiar in the way he stood. Just then, the door to the warehouse opened, and a young man dressed in the clothes of a common workman came running in. He was excited as he hurried up to the other man. They spoke in low voices, but I could make out their conversation easily in the silence of the warehouse. To my horror, the first voice was that of Professor Davies.

"Well?" asked Davies.

"It's done, sir, just like you told me. I gave the note to the constable, and 'e took it straight off," the other man said excitedly.

"Thank you, Billy, now go keep watch outside. I expect our guest to arrive shortly. Make sure you don't intercept him, but inform me at once when he appears."

"Yes, sir!" The young man took off out the door, making sure to close it behind him. Davies watched him go, walked down the stairs, and came toward Agatha and me.

"Good morning, Dr. Collins, you no doubt remember me?" he said.

"Duh." I felt strangely calm, and Davies didn't scare me a bit. "How did you get away from the Andaman Islands?"

"That is none of your business." He lit a cigarette.

"Why did you bring us here?" I asked.

"So I could have my revenge. You were there the day I warned Jeremy, and I always keep to my word." He smiled maliciously.

"Look, it doesn't have to be this way. You're unstable, you should seek medical help," I said. Agatha stirred beside me, no doubt awakened by our voices.

"Perhaps you are correct, doctor, but the only problem with that is I don't want help; I want revenge." He punctuated his last sentence with a cloud of cigarette smoke.

I stared at him incredulously. "Wow, you really do need help."

He laughed. "It seems it is too late for that. I have had the opportunity to perform a little research on my adopted brother during the past few months, and I have turned up some interesting facts. You might even say I am an expert on him now. Although he is a formidable young man, his sanity is obviously unstable, and I believe I know just how to drive him over the edge."

"What are you going to do to him?" asked Agatha.

"Ah, sister dearest, I am so glad you are awake now. I regret that we never knew each other as children since I left before you were born, but it does make it easier for my conscience when my vengeance is complete. Congratulations on your recent wedding by the way. However, I am disappointed with your choice of groom. It does tangle you hopelessly into this affair."

"My husband is a far better man than you could ever hope to be."

"I seriously doubt that. Your husband is a coward."

"My husband is kind-hearted, which is easily mistaken for timidity."

"I do doubt that, and I am sure you will in time come to realize that I am correct. However, this is beside the point, and we haven't much time until Jeremy arrives. I believe you asked me what I was going to do to him. It is quite simple; I plan to murder you both in his presence."

"You'll be hanged for this," I said as deep loathing welled within me. "You'll never get away with it."

"My dear sir, it matters not what happens to me. Once I have the pleasure of revenge, my purpose will be fulfilled, and then I will welcome death."

"You disgusting creature!" Agatha said in a dangerously quiet voice. "You could have been a great man, but you have dropped far from your potential. The gates of hell are opening before you, and I hope you suffer well at the hands of the one to whom you have forfeited your soul!" Davies stared angrily at her and then slapped her hard across the face, which knocked her to the ground. I tried to stand, but he pointed a gun at me.

"I should kill you for speaking to me so, my dear sister. Where on earth did you learn such unladylike speech? As it is, one more word out of you and your husband will suffer for your insolence." He held the gun against my head as a warning to Agatha, and she shot daggers with her eyes at him from where she lay on the floor, a bruise forming where he had struck her. He shoved me back against the crates and roughly hauled her back up to her former position.

Just then, the young man rushed into the building in a flurry of excitement.

"He's here, Professor, sir! I saw him comin' up the dock like the devil himself was chasing him."

"Thank you, Billy, you've done well. Here's your pay." Davies gave the young man a handful of sovereigns, much to his delight. "Now, make yourself scarce. I shan't need you any more."

"Yes, sir!" Billy disappeared out a back door located under the balcony. Davies checked his gun to make sure that it was loaded and stuck it back into his pocket. We heard the sound of the door being opened, and an evil sneer crept across Davies' face that sickened me.

"Well, well, well, if it isn't Jeremy Hawkins come down from his lofty heights to mingle with his lowly criminal brother. Please, come in! We've been expecting you."

I looked over. A wave of relief washed over me at the sight of Hawkins' familiar red hair and pale face. He wore a calm expression. His eyes never wavered from Davies'.

"Collins, Aggie, are you unharmed?" he asked when he was near us.

"We're fine." I replied.

"Good. Now then, Stephen, I fear you have committed a social blunder. It is not generally deemed polite to kidnap one's guests." Hawkins chose his words carefully, and Davies smirked humorlessly.

"I see you haven't lost your mastery of speech. I trust you didn't bring any unwelcome guests with you."

"I do not believe that the police would be beneficial under such circumstances."

"Excellent! You have some common sense at least. You must realize why I have brought you here."

"Yes, but I assure you that you needn't retain Collins nor Agatha; they will get you nothing."

"On the contrary, they will get me everything. You underestimated me, my brother. I can see it in your eyes that you were not expecting me to act with such cleverness. Well, you are not the only who has a turn for strategizing. I have, after all, planned what Scotland Yard acclaims some of the most daring heists of the century." Davies paced slowly back and forth while he spoke. "Ever since I saw you in that courtroom, I've been planning my revenge. When I was on the Andaman Islands, a truly wretched place, my mind found a scheme that was absolutely perfect. I knew that death would not be enough punishment after all you have done to me. No, I needed to destroy you. So, I made a study of Jeremy Hawkins, and I found a weakness." He ceased pacing and continued cuttingly, "You ruined me, Jeremy. From the very moment you came into my life, you ruined me. I finally bested you in one area, though; I became lord of the criminal underworld. But you stole that from me as well. Now, my own sister even despises me. I have nothing, thanks to you."

"You committed the crimes, Stephen, I had no choice but to do what I did," Hawkins replied.

"To do what you did, eh? Well this is what I have to do, and I hope you enjoy it immensely."

Davies had been pointing his gun at me the entire time, but to my alarm, he directed the gun at Agatha and shot her.

"Agatha! No!" I heard myself shout, but I was only aware of the horrified look on her face as the life drained out of her. I had been rubbing the ropes around my wrists against the rough edge of the crate behind me for hours, and with a rush of adrenaline, I broke through the remaining strands to catch my wife before she fell to the floor. She died in my arms.

"If I cannot have the love of my sister, then neither shall you," Davies exclaimed. "Her blood is on your hands now. How does it feel to fail, Jeremy? You no doubt had one of your little strategies planned before you came here, but it was to no avail. How does it feel to fail?" He was almost dancing with glee.

Hawkins stared at Agatha in disbelief. "Damn you, Stephen. Damn you!" Hawkins leapt at Davies, but found his adversary prepared for the battle. Davies kicked Hawkins' leg where he had been shot. Hawkins collapsed with a yelp, Davies picked him up and pitched him over a crate where he landed heavily on the other side. Consumed with rage, I had ceased to think and was only acting at that point. I unbound my legs and threw myself at Davies, grabbing him by the throat as tightly as I could. He was a better fighter than I and knocked me to the ground easily. I found myself facing the barrel of his gun. He snarled and shot me in the head before Hawkins could react.

There was a blinding flash of light as the bullet made contact with my forehead. Darkness engulfed me.

WHEN I REGAINED consciousness, I was amazed by the mere fact that I was alive. The next thought that went through my mind was concern for Hawkins. I sat up. Instead of the interior of the warehouse, I was looking at trees. I was back in the forest clearing in Tenino where I had first been transported into the 19th century!

I stood up slowly and looked around. The clearing looked almost exactly as I had left it, but it smelled different. Instead of the warm, somewhat spicy odor of summertime, the air smelled cold and had that clean smell that comes after it has rained.

Bewildered, I thought perhaps that I had fallen asleep in the clearing and dreamed up the whole experience and that it had rained while I was unconscious. Of course, this was a poor explanation, but I needed to understand what had happened to me. But then I noticed I was wearing the same black trousers, waistcoat, white shirt, boots, and coat that I had been wearing in the warehouse. It can't be! Stunned, my gaze fell on the tablet in the center of the clearing. I turned without another thought and ran madly.

I made it out of the forest, leaned against a tree for support, fingered my wedding ring, and considered my situation. I had really been in 19th-century England. I had married a young lady named Agatha. I had watched her die. I had been shot in the head. I quickly touched my forehead where I had been shot and felt nothing. I was confused and overwhelmed. I was too devastated to think.

I walked to my brother's house with my eyes to the ground and heaviness in my heart. I didn't notice anything or anyone around me. My sole goal was to make it home. I stepped onto the porch. The door was unlocked. I entered. I stood in the entry hall and heard from the living room to my right a voice call out, "Who's there?"

"It's just me, Richard."

"Andrew? Oh my God! Andrew!"

Richard ran up to me and embraced me tightly. I hesitated, and then returned his embrace warmly. The strength of my older brother felt warm and safe somehow. By this time, his wife and daughters had joined us from the other room. Lisa was crying, and the girls kept shouting, "Uncle Andrew! Uncle Andrew!"

"How long have I been gone?" I asked as I pulled away from my brother.

"You've been gone for over a year. The police gave you up for dead quite some time ago, but I knew you were alive!" Richard said.

"Oh." Apparently, the same amount of time had passed in

Tenino as I had experienced in London, but this didn't surprise me at all. I wished that it had been different, because now I had to explain my disappearance.

"Man, I'm glad to see that you're alright! You are alright, aren't you? There's blood on your shirt."

I examined my shirt, and found bloodstains on the front. When I realized that it was Agatha's blood, I had to fight to keep my emotions in check. "Oh, it's, uh, from an old battle."

"It looks like you've had an interesting time wherever you've been. What happened to you?"

I hesitated a moment to make up a story about being kidnapped by a hobo in the woods, but then decided to say simply that I couldn't remember what happened. I could tell by the look on Richard and Lisa's faces that they didn't entirely believe me, but I didn't know what else to say.

"Amnesia?" My brother asked.

"Rick, maybe we should have a doctor take a look at him," Lisa suggested.

"No, I'm fine. I think I hit my head or something is all."

"Are you sure?" Richard asked.

"Sure I'm sure. I am a doctor, remember?"

"Maybe you should get a second opinion," said Lisa.

"You're a psychologist, not a doctor," Richard pointed out.

"Well, it doesn't really matter, right? At least I'm back anyway. I'll feel better after I take a shower and get some sleep."

"Well, ok. You know where the shower is. We left your room exactly as it was. It just didn't seem right to change it," Richard said.

"Thanks." I mechanically gave my nieces each a hug and told them I had missed them, saluted Lisa with a bow like Hawkins had taught me, shook hands with my brother, and walked upstairs. I went into the bathroom so I could wash my hands, found that I needed a towel, and went back to the top of stairs where the linen closet was located. Richard and Lisa were speaking in low voices.

"Richard, something's wrong with him. I'm worried," Lisa said.

"I know, honey, but we can't force him to talk about it if he doesn't want to," Richard replied.

"I guess you're right. I think he was lying about not remembering."

"Oh, I'm sure he was. He's never been able to lie his entire life."

"What do we do?"

"For the time being, let's just leave him alone and see how he gets on. When he's ready to talk, we'll be here for him."

"Ok. What was with that bow he did?"

"I don't know. It was kind of weird. Maybe he stayed with a well-mannered family?"

"Yeah, but I doubt it." They left the entryway, and I couldn't hear them anymore. I smiled somewhat ruefully at the thought that my brother knew I was lying even though he wouldn't have believed the truth. I grabbed a towel and went into the bathroom.

After I had depleted the hot water tank of its steaming contents, I retired to my room and fell into a deep sleep.

✳ CHAPTER XVI

THE NEXT FEW WEEKS WERE THE MOST difficult of my life. If you have ever lost a loved one or everything you hold dear you would understand. I had lost not just my wife—torn apart from me so quickly—I had lost my entire life. I was numb with shock, disbelief, and grief. I had disturbing dreams of blood-stained floors and broken violins. At times, I awoke convinced that I heard Agatha screaming my name.

My brother kept a close eye on me. He suggested once that I see his friend, Spencer Young, who was a counselor. I declined and told him I felt awkward about one psychologist seeking help from another. He didn't press the issue. Richard also wanted to write an article about my reappearance, but I begged him not to. I didn't want to bring any attention to myself, and I knew there would be questions regarding what happened. I was also afraid that an investigation might reveal the tablet that sent me to the 19th century and the dire consequences of that revelation.

I occasionally considered returning to the tablet, but I didn't have the heart to go. It was too painful. I forced myself to live every day, even though it seemed as though nothing could alleviate my sorrow.

The days slowly passed. November turned to December. Christmas was coming, but the celebrations held no cheer for me.

From the sidelines, I watched as everyone around me enjoyed the holiday spirit. I was in an emotional void and couldn't think or feel. At times, I tried to convince myself that nothing had happened to me, and I began to wonder where I had been a year ago. I was like a zombie as I dragged myself through each day. I couldn't stand to be alone, but I was estranged from my family. I felt like a piece of wood tethered to a rock sunken at the bottom of the ocean while everyone else floated gaily on the surface. I could see them up there, wanted to be up there, but I just couldn't free myself to join them.

Christmas Eve arrived. At the end of the day, after my nieces had been sent to bed, Richard, Lisa, and I sat in the living room. Lisa crocheted, Richard perused some documents, and I stared out the window at the driving rain—typical Washington winter weather. If I had been able and willing to think about it, I would have missed the scenic countryside of Surrey and its beautiful snow. I would have remembered what it felt like to build an army of snowmen and battling the domestic staff with an artillery of snowballs. I would have remembered what it felt like to hold Agatha in my arms.

Richard broke the silence.

"Hey, guys! You should listen to this, it's pretty interesting." He was holding some photocopies of what looked like newspaper articles.

"What is it?" Lisa asked.

"It's an old, very old, article. One of my co-workers has a bunch of them, and he gave me some copies. These articles are always so fascinating."

"Yeah, sure dear," she yawned.

"Hmm, well you'll share my opinion in a moment. This is an article that apparently has to do with a relative of ours. His name is Andrew."

"Oh really?" She looked up from her project with interest.

"Well, it appears that this guy, Andrew Collins, disappeared one night kind of like our Andrew."

"Weird!" She said simply. I took notice.

"Get this, though, they found his wife dead in a warehouse later that same night."

"When was this? Where was this?" I asked, trying not to sound too excited.

"Umm, the exact date was cut off, but I think it was somewhere around 1890. My co-worker said that at least one of these was from London, but I'm not sure which."

My hands were shaking.

Richard continued, "Yeah, it's kind of weird. Apparently a guy named Professor Stephen Elliot Davies, a well-respected scientist, was found in the warehouse along with the brother of the dead wife. Professor Davies confessed to having murdered both Collins and his wife, but he claimed that he didn't know what happened to the body of Collins. The guy's obviously lying. He probably threw the body into the river or something, and was about to do the same with the wife."

"But why would he lie about that if he already confessed to murder?" Lisa asked.

"I hadn't thought of that. Maybe—"

"What happened to him? To Professor Davies I mean." I interjected.

"I'm not sure. I don't have that article here. The guy probably hanged for his crimes. I mean, he killed two people. I wonder what his motive was."

"Revenge," I replied quietly—more to myself than to Richard and Lisa.

"It was a cruel world, even back then. I mean, just look at Jack the Ripper!" Richard exclaimed.

"Is sure was." Lisa replied. Their conversation continued, but I didn't hear a word of it. I sat back into my chair, feeling uneasy. My mind raced when Richard broke the silence once more.

"Hey, Andrew?"

"What?"

"Can you stir the fire? I think it's starting to die."

"Yeah, sure." I absentmindedly got out of my chair and walked to the woodstove.

"That flue is kind of tricky, be careful with it," Richard warned.

"Ok." I said, not really comprehending what he had said. I mechanically grabbed the fire poker, shoved the flue all the way in, and opened the door with a rough tug. A cloud of wood smoke bellowed into the room, and I had a flashback.

I was back in the sitting room of Montague Street. I had never noticed, but that room had always smelled faintly of wood smoke, even if Mrs. Montgomery burned charcoal. The smell of wood smoke was stronger than normal. Hawkins, Agatha, Mr. Blessington, Mrs. Montgomery, and I were standing in a half circle, all of us holding crystal glasses. Mrs. Montgomery raised hers and simply said, "To family," and we all echoed her sentiment. It was Christmas day, and I had been drunk the previous night. I could almost feel my head throb again, and the smell of the champagne made me sick to my stomach. However, the same feeling of contentment and belonging that I had felt that day returned to me in a rush, and happiness washed over me even as I vividly recalled and sensed everything that had happened a year ago.

"Andrew! Andrew! For God's sake open the flue!" Richard was shouting at me.

"Oh!" I quickly pulled the flue open. The fire had died completely, and the room was full of smoke. Lisa opened a window while a smoke detector went off, and Richard waved his papers in front of the beeping alarm, trying to silence it. Throughout the chaos, I still kneeled in front of the stove, desperately trying to hold on to every detail of Agatha's face from my flashback. It had all been so powerful. Tears came to my eyes, and I sobbed.

It hit me! I didn't belong in this century. I had found contentment in the 19th century, and that was where I belonged. I needed to go home! But with a pang of sadness, I recalled Agatha's death and how less bright it would be without her. Briefly, I wondered if I could live without my beloved a time period where everything would remind me of the one I lost. Yet, I would have Hawkins—my dear friend. Hawkins! I saw through my despair to what I wanted to do.

Richard and Lisa were vanquishing the last traces of smoke from the air. I stood, bounded to my room, changed into my British suit, and ran downstairs out the front door. As I sprinted down the street, I heard Richard's voice behind me, and I felt guilty for just leaving him like that. However, if I paused to explain, he would stop me. I ran even harder. Besides, if this didn't work, I would be back in a minute anyway.

The daylight had disappeared hours ago, and I thought I would have trouble finding my way. However, my feet knew where I was going even if I couldn't see. I finally made it to the mysterious clearing that I had first encountered over a year ago. The rain pelted me, and I shivered as a blast of wind wrapped me in its icy grip. I could just make out the tablet in the center and I walked to it, still panting hard from my wild sprint. I dropped to my hands and knees on the squishy earth and rubbed my hand across the smooth surface of the stone, feeling the grooves of the inscriptions and praying that it would work. The vine patterns along the border and the etching of the eyes started to glow. The blinding flash of light came quickly, and I was knocked unconscious.

CHAPTER XVII

W HEN I OPENED MY EYES, I WAS LYING
in the same dirt lane as last time. I sat up slowly
and let the dizziness and nausea pass before I stood. The unpleasant
symptoms passed quicker than last time, and I noticed that they
weren't nearly as potent.

The street was deserted, and an icy breeze whipped by me. I
heard a cat shriek and glanced over at the small cemetery with
superstitious dread. The sky overhead was dark and clouded, and I
shivered as a few snowflakes lazily drifted by me in the light of the
gas lamps. I stood and hastily walked from the lane to the main
road, which still had some pedestrians and traffic on it. A troupe
of Christmas carolers beneath a gas lamp sang of the Savior's birth.
I sighed with relief, glad to be home, and found a cab to take me
to Montague Street.

When I arrived at the house, I saw that there were no lights in
the windows. Curious but not alarmed, I went to the door, knocked
loudly, and waited. After three more knocks, there still came no
answer. I became alarmed. I tried the door. It was locked. I
remembered my keys and unlocked the door.

The house was very cold when I entered. Somewhere in the
stillness of the house, I heard a mouse scurry, but no other sound.
I shut the door and was engulfed in darkness. I found a few candles

and some matches in a drawer in the entryway table and lit a candle.

With light, the first thing I noticed was the filthiness of the floor. There was a layer of dust on everything. I quickly examined the lower story. It was deserted. Mrs. Montgomery's room was empty as was the dining room. All of her belongings were gone. This puzzled me. Why would Mrs. Montgomery leave this house? I went into the kitchen and was appalled by what I saw. The stove was covered with dirty pots, and there was food rotting on the table. A few more mice scurried away from me as I went into the scullery. The sink was loaded with dirty dishes. It seemed impossible that our good landlady would let her house sink to such a state, and I couldn't account for this at all. Confused, I went upstairs to see what I could find.

The sitting room door was partially ajar, and I entered cautiously. It was a complete disaster! The floor illuminated by my candle was littered with random objects, and the majority appeared to be broken. I carefully stepped through the rubble to the gas jets over the fireplace and lit them. I blew out my candle and set it on the mantle, which had been relieved of its usual residents. I looked at the floor by my feet and found the objects—including the clock which was now smashed—in a heap. It was as if someone had just shoved them off the mantelpiece.

The books that usually occupied the shelves on the far wall were strewn about the room as if someone had thrown them randomly. A few of them had also had some of their leaves torn out, and these were mingled with Hawkins' papers on the floor. The upholstery on both armchairs had been shredded, and another unfortunate chair had been smashed against the table. The couch cushions were lying in pieces on the floor. I knew that Hawkins liked having the sitting room in a state of chaos, but this was too much even for him. The room looked like a burglar had ransacked it.

I went to Hawkins' room and looked in. It also was a mess and deserted. Perhaps the house had been burgled. But if that was so, where were its occupants? According to the dust, no one had been in the house recently. It didn't make any sense.

As I walked out of Hawkins' room, I found his violin half buried under some papers and a broken tea set. The unique instrument was intact and didn't seem to be damaged. I picked it up carefully and gently set it on the sofa. I wanted to check upstairs and tried to find one of the oil lamps that usually sat in this room.

I found one oil lamp on the floor, undamaged but empty; another one was lying in pieces below where it had struck the wall; and the third had a crack running its length. Not to be deterred, I grabbed my candle and relit it before heading into the hallway and up the stairs. The upper rooms provided no clues as to what had happened. They had been swept clean. I returned to the sitting room and pondered what to do.

The house seemed to have been abandoned for several weeks, and it didn't look as though anyone was coming back to it. Where were Mrs. Montgomery and Hawkins? Why would they leave the house in such a state? I decided to find Mr. Thomas Blessington, hoping that he hadn't disappeared also.

I extinguished the gaslights, took my candle, and descended the dark staircase. I put out my light and left it on the entryway table before exiting the abandoned house and locking the door behind me. I walked to Baker Street to Thomas Blessington's residence.

To my relief, there were lights on in his house, which seemed especially cheerful after the dark windows I had just left. A maid answered the door when I knocked, and I was shown to the somewhat bare sitting room. The entire house, or at least what I had seen of it, had a plain look to it, which complemented its landlady immensely. As I walked up the uncarpeted stairs, I noticed the bare walls with their yellowed wallpaper and couldn't help but think of how Mrs. Montgomery could have made this house a little less foreboding.

Blessington was seated in front of a roaring fire and stared into its depths motionless like a statue with a gloomy expression that was different from his usual manner. He leapt out of his chair as soon as the maid announced me. Thomas Blessington is not a faint-hearted man, but I was sure for a moment that he was about to faint. He plopped back into his chair with a look of astonishment.

"Dr. Collins?"

"Hello, Thomas!" I said cheerfully. "How are you today?"

He burst out into a laugh that wasn't as hearty as I had remembered.

"They told me you were dead, and then you come a-walking through my door? How is it that you came to be here, doctor?"

"It's a long story, but I didn't die. I found myself somewhere a long way from here, and I only just made it back today." Blessington didn't know my story, and I didn't want to tell it to him. He was a very trusting soul, but I didn't think he would believe me.

"Ah, I see. It is nice to be seeing you again, sir. Please, have a seat! Would you like something to drink?"

I declined his offer and sat down in the chair next to him. "What's happened since I left? I went to Montague Street before I came here, and it seemed abandoned."

"That's a sad business it is. I hate to be the one to tell you, seeing as how you were so close to her, but dear Mrs. Montgomery passed away."

"She's d-dead?" I stuttered. "How? When?"

"We figure it was grief that did her in. She was taken ill when she heard about you and Agatha, and she never recovered. It wasn't long after that the poor woman passed on."

"That's horrible! She was such a good person." I couldn't help feel somewhat responsible for her death.

"Aye, she was indeed."

"Wait, so what about Hawkins? He isn't dead is he?"

"Mr. Hawkins? No, he's still around. I don't see too much of him these days. Mrs. Montgomery's death was a hard blow after what happened to you and Miss Agatha. He spends most of his time in the pub I reckon."

"He drinks? Hawkins drinks? Good grief how could things be any worse?" I sat back in my chair, overwhelmed by all of this.

Mrs. Montgomery and Agatha were both dead, Hawkins was a drunk, and Mr. Blessington was no longer the cheerful fellow I had known him to be. London seemed a nightmare, and I wasn't sure what to do. However, I knew that I must get my friend and pull him out of the bottle into which he had climbed.

"Thomas, can you take me to him?"

"To Mr. Hawkins you mean? Yes, I think I know where he would be this time of night. Come with me, sir."

I HAD THE OPPORTUNITY to observe Blessington a bit as we drove through London's snowy streets that night. He was very quiet, which was unusual, and he didn't laugh as easily as he once had. He was a far cry from his former buoyant spirit. His physical appearance had also suffered with his moods. He was thinner than before, and his face had lost its healthy shade in favor of one that was far paler.

Blessington took me to a seedy pub in the East End of London. As could be expected from its location, the pub was crowded with the shadiest-looking characters imaginable. Many of them stared at us as we walked in. The smell hit me the hardest—tobacco smoke, alcohol, poor hygiene, and general filth. A bit of garland strung around the doorway seemed more of an insult to the season than a decoration. Hawkins was a fairly sophisticated fellow, and it surprised me that he would be here. He had certainly fallen far if he had chosen to be in such a place.

"Are you sure he's in here?" I asked Blessington.

"Yes sir. That's him over there in fact."

I followed Blessington's gaze to where a solitary man sat in the corner. He was slouched over a table with his head bowed and a mug in his hand. I had to look twice before I realized that it really was Hawkins. Blessington steered his large frame through the crowded room, and I followed in his wake.

Hawkins swayed over his beer. His typical unruly hair had grown long and sat on his head like a shaggy mat of red moss. His face was dirty and unshaven and dirt was under his nails, which was appalling when one considered his former love of personal hygiene. He was dressed in a tan waistcoat, black trousers, and a tattered brown overcoat. His pocket watch wasn't in his waistcoat pocket.

If you have ever seen a great painting thrown carelessly into the mud, than you can understand the great pity and sadness I felt as I looked at what used to be a great man. He had been trodden down, and I feared that his strong will was broken at last.

"We should get him out of here. He doesn't belong here," I said to Blessington.

"Yes, I agree, but where should we take him?"

"Umm, can we take him back to your place?"

"Yes." Blessington turned to Hawkins and shook him gently. "Mr. Hawkins, sir? Mr. Hawkins, it's time to leave."

Hawkins stirred and squinted at Blessington. When I saw his eyes, it was all I could do to not recoil in horror. Where they had shined with a bright spark that bespoke of the keen mind tucked away in his skull, they were now dull and listless. There was no fire in them anymore. He was a broken man. I could only hope that there was a chance he could be fixed.

Blessington pulled Hawkins to his feet. Quite drunk, Hawkins swayed and fell against Blessington.

"I say, Thomas Blessington, is that you?" he asked.

"Yes, sir, it's me." Blessington hauled him upright once more, and I grabbed his other arm. Hawkins looked up at me in recognition and surprise. He steadied himself against Blessington as he studied me and then passed out.

"Oops," I said. "Let's get him out of here. This place gives me the creeps."

Blessington easily lifted Hawkins' slender frame and slung him over his shoulder. We made our way through the crowded room as quickly as we could out to the cold air. We located a four-wheeler, and I was glad when we were on our way back to Baker Street.

Our trip there and back took a couple of hours, and the clock struck twelve when we were once again in Blessington's sitting room. We laid Hawkins on the couch without undressing him, except for his soaked and muddy boots.

"Is there anything more we should do for him, doctor?" Blessington asked.

"No, I think it would be best if we just let him sleep it off."

"There's a spare bedroom upstairs that you are welcome to if you wish, sir."

"Thanks, but I think I'll stay here if you don't mind. I want to be nearby when he wakes up. By the way, merry Christmas, Thomas." He smiled and then left the room.

Blessington went to bed. I pulled my armchair to the end of the couch and hoped that I too could fall asleep. Although I was tired, my mind denied me rest. I pondered all that had happened since my departure, and it was all so horrible that I wept. The situation was dire, and there was nothing I could do about it.

I fell into a light sleep around 2:30 that morning and awoke around five when my sobered friend revived. Hawkins sat up on the couch and looked around slowly, no doubt trying to get his bearings.

"Hawkins," I said softly. Hawkins started violently and looked at me in the dim light with open wonder.

"Good heavens!" he exclaimed. "I must be drunker than I supposed."

"No, I think you're actually sobering up by now."

"In that case, I need a drink." He made a move as if to rise.

"Oh no you don't!" I said vehemently. "I'm not going to sit by and watch while you throw yourself away."

"Well then, I am afraid you'll have to look away."

"You don't believe I'm really here do you?"

"I have never hallucinated before, and I admit that it is rather more lifelike than I would have thought." He studied me curiously as he said this and seemed to be talking to himself more than to me.

"You're not hallucinating. I'm really here."

"I suppose it is fitting that it should be you who haunts me. I am, after all, responsible for your death."

"Hawkins—"

"It is a pity that you died; you and dear Aggie. Oh! I did try to protect her, but I could not. And now I have killed you both." Although you would think it natural for someone to cry when he said something like this, Hawkins didn't show any signs of emotion. He just sort of stared off into space and spoke as if he were merely commenting on a book he had read. I shuddered as I remembered the void I had felt after losing everything and could understand that Hawkins might be feeling something similar.

"For the love of Ronald Reagan will you please listen to me? I'm not dead!"

"I am not entirely convinced that you are a hallucination," Hawkins said. "I am rather inclined to think this is a dream, and I will soon wake up and find myself back in the pub."

I threw my arms up in frustration and paced in front of the couch. How was I to convince him? It is rare that inspiration strikes me, but at that moment it struck hard. "Hawkins, forgive me for this, but I don't know how else to convince you." I then slapped him across the face as hard as I could.

"Collins, that was completely unnecessary!" He paused and looked at me with a different expression, and I knew I had gotten through to him.

"There, you see? Now, what man in a dream can slap you?" I said.

"Good heavens, so you are real. It is so difficult to tell reality from fantasy these days, I hope you will excuse my skepticism."

"Only if you forgive me for slapping you." I chuckled and sat down next to him on the couch.

He broke out into a wide smile and then gripped me by the arm. "Collins, it is wonderful to see you again! What happened to you?"

"It is wonderful to be seen by you again. I was beginning to think I wouldn't be able to convince you that I'm alive. Hawkins, when I was shot in the head, I became unconscious and woke up in the clearing in the 21st century. My brother Richard said I had been gone over a year. I was in a stupor—couldn't think, didn't know what to think. After losing Agatha, you, my life in London,

I just felt numb. Several horrible weeks passed. But then I had a flashback of my life in London—with you and Agatha—and I knew I needed to come back because it's my home."

Hawkins' smile slowly faded from his face, and he fidgeted like one who is embarrassed.

"I feel it is necessary to apologize for the state you found me in. It was a very poor way to greet you I am sure."

"It's fine. I've felt like crawling into a bottle myself a few times."

"You have my solemn word that it shall never happen again."

We sat in silence for a few minutes. "What happens now, Hawkins?" I asked. "Are we just going to waste the rest of our lives as lonely bachelors?"

"In other words, are you suggesting that we do nothing? You know very well that that would be a complete waste."

❋ CHAPTER XVIII

BLESSINGTON WOKE UP AROUND seven and we had breakfast. Both Blessington and Hawkins seemed nearer to their former selves as they bantered back and forth, but there was still a difference. It was good just to have them back.

After we finished eating, I thanked Blessington for his services and thought that it would be best for Hawkins and me to return to our former dwelling. Hawkins refused at first, but I convinced him. He wasn't nearly as masterful as I remembered, and I was surprised that he didn't put up more of a fuss. Blessington offered to accompany us, but I told him that it wouldn't be necessary.

Hawkins and I walked home. The weather had cleared up since the previous night, and all the evidence of the snow had been erased. The sun shone brightly on the wet pavement. Although the air in London never smelled clean, it smelled less polluted than normal.

Hawkins walked slowly—still with a pronounced limp—which was a nice break for me since I normally had to hurry to keep up with him. He stared at the ground in resolute silence. I thought about dragging him into a conversation, but I eventually decided that this would be unwise and enjoyed the morning around me instead. I had strolled with Hawkins many times, but it was strange to walk in complete silence. Our strange walk didn't last long though, for we soon arrived at the late Mrs. Montgomery's former residence.

"I am not so sure this is a wise decision." Hawkins said to me when we reached Montague Street.

"Why not?" I asked.

He merely sighed and unlocked the front door without explaining himself. I shrugged off his statement. The house looked even more forlorn in the daylight than it had by candlelight. The layer of dust that covered everything robbed the house of its colors and replaced them with a drab grayish hue. The lack of color seemed almost fitting in view of recent events. It was as if the house itself was mourning its late mistress.

Hawkins walked up the stairs quickly and paused at the top before he pushed open the door to the sitting room.

"Good God, it's even worse than I remembered," he whispered.

I pushed past Hawkins and made my way through the disaster area to open the blinds. The light from the outdoors banished the shadows from the room and made it seem like less of a monster.

"How did this happen?" I asked.

"I would rather not discuss it," Hawkins said sheepishly.

"Ok."

He cleared his throat and set about straightening the room. I joined him.

"What's going to happen to the house?"

"It belongs to me now. Mrs. Montgomery left it to me in her will."

"Oh, neat. What are you going to do with it?"

"I will most likely continue to live here. I don't think I could possibly leave it; it has been my residence for so long. I will hire a housekeeper and a maid. You are more than welcome to stay as long as you wish."

"Thanks. I don't know where else I would go."

"To Surrey, of course. As Agatha's husband, all of her property is entailed to you."

"What?" I hadn't considered this. "But I can't live there! It just won't be the same without her."

Hawkins shrugged. "It is your decision."

We fell silent as we continued to clean the sitting room. Cleaning is a mundane task, and I was able to think about what had happened. I had an idea, which I dismissed at first because it was crazy. But it seemed so thoroughly crazy that it might just work. I turned to Hawkins in excitement.

"Hawkins! Let's change the past!" I half shouted.

"I beg your pardon?" He asked, more than somewhat incredulous.

"Let's change the past! Look, I can move between the past and the future, right? Why can't I go to a specific point in the past and prevent Davies from doing what he did?"

"And what would be the point of this?" He paused to toss the broken clock onto the trash pile. "What has happened has happened, Collins. We cannot change it."

"I can't believe you just said that! I thought you would leap at the opportunity to set things straight."

"Perhaps you thought incorrectly."

"Yeah, I guess so." I paused, and anger welled up inside of me. "You coward." He turned toward me with an indignant expression in his lifeless eyes.

"No, Collins, I am no coward, I am a realist. There is a marked difference between the two. I have accepted what happened, as terrible as it is, and I am moving on with my life. I suggest you do the same."

"Realist? More like a pessimist. Look, it doesn't have to be this way! There is a chance we can fix what happened! You owe it to Agatha and Mrs. Montgomery to at least try."

"I am sorry, old fellow, but I cannot. Whatever you will do, you must do it without me."

"Fine." I stomped out of the room, grabbed my coat and hat, and left the house in a fury.

I stormed down Montague Street with my hands jammed into my pockets and scowl on my face. In my opinion, Hawkins was being cowardly, and it angered me that he wouldn't even try. I needed his help, as I couldn't accomplish my task without him. A part of me was angry at me, for I had a vague feeling that his mental state was my fault. Davies' words in the warehouse came back to me, and with a sick feeling I realized that he had achieved his revenge—my friend was a prisoner in his own mind.

I stayed on Montague Street, just pacing up and down until the sun began to fall from its zenith, and the western horizon began to grow rosy. I could see my breath in the chilly air, and the people who passed me gave me a wide berth. I'm not one for holding a grudge, and I quickly lamented my harsh words. I decided to return and apologize to my friend. The sitting room was spotless when I entered, but Hawkins was nowhere to be seen.

"Hawkins!" I called. I heard movement from behind his bedroom door, and he emerged a second later. His appearance was as spotless as the room. I was encouraged to see him cleaned up.

Hawkins didn't say a word to me at first, but stood there and played with the cuffs of his shirt with a chagrined air. I was about to speak, but he cut me off and spoke first. "Collins, I have thought a great deal about what you said, and I believe I understand why you said it. I owe you an apology for my insensitivity."

"I'm sorry too. I didn't mean to snap. It seems kind of childish to yell at you when I didn't get my way."

"You were right though, I do owe them something."

I was almost afraid to hope, but my spirits rose slightly. "So, you'll help me?"

"I will assist you even if it leads to death." He said with a smile.

"Yes! That's the Hawkins I know! So where do we start?"

"I believe a certain dirt lane in the city would be the ideal place to begin."

"Good! Let's go!"

THERE WAS NOTHING particularly remarkable about this small dirt lane. It merely served to provide a path between two parallel cobblestone streets. It was really more of an alley than a lane in this respect. I went to the spot in the path where I had first found myself upon waking after my two journeys to London.

"Do you suppose the tablet in the 21st century has a counterpart in London? This could, however, be just a random location I suppose," Hawkins mused. "If the former was true, why would you have traveled from the warehouse to the clearing after being shot? You really should have found yourself far apart from earth."

"Maybe it's like when you're playing a video game and you get sent back to the beginning of a level when you run out of hit points," I ventured.

"I haven't the slightest idea what a video game is, but that somehow makes sense to me."

Hawkins walked to the fence of the cemetery and stared at it while chewing on the stem of his pipe. He was obviously pondering his next move, and I joined him in studying the headstones. Graveyards have always elicited a feeling of respect and awe in me. As I stared at the stone markers where so many people were laid to rest, I couldn't help but shudder at the mystery of death.

"What do you think happens to us when we die?" I whispered.

"That is an intriguing question. There are some who believe that a person's spirit leaves the body, others believe that we are sent back in another form. I knew a man once who swore that his wife's spirit haunted his pub. However, I must concur with the belief that our spirits go to dwell apart from this earth."

"You mean like heaven or hell?"

"I suppose so."

"I've heard that some people are accidentally buried alive. That must be so freaky; buried beneath so much dirt for so long— just like a rock or something."

Hawkins ceased masticating his pipe stem and brightened as one who has an idea. "That's it! How blind I've been! He shoved his pipe into his overcoat pocket and seeing a few pickaxes and shovels leaning against the fence nearby, he took one of the latter and went out into the lane.

"What are you doing?" I asked.

"What a fool I've been! It's all so obvious!"

"What is?"

"It is as you said, 'buried beneath so much dirt for so long—just like a rock or something.' That's the answer!"

"I don't understand."

"Collins, the tablet is buried beneath the surface of this lane!"

"How do you know?"

"Call it a hunch if you will, but I am absolutely certain. Besides, there is no harm done if I am mistaken. Come now, we must dig!"

Hawkins drove his shovel zealously into the damp, compacted earth of the lane. I also grabbed a shovel and joined him in excavating the lane. We dug into the unsuspecting earth vigorously, and people who passed by stared at us curiously. I was in terror that one of them might at any moment fetch a police officer, but all such thoughts were banished when after digging less than a foot into the center of the lane, my shovel struck something hard.

"I think I found something!" I cried. I quickly shoveled off enough dirt to sufficiently reveal the object and dropped to my hands and knees to finish cleaning it off. Hawkins, who was as sweaty and dirty as me, practically threw himself next to me to help. It didn't take long to clean it off, and there before us lay a rectangular stone that made my heart leap for joy.

The London tablet was basically the same as the Tenino one in shape and size, but its decorations differed slightly. The embellishments on the borders of the London tablet lacked the vine pattern of its counterpart and had a more orderly design instead. It reminded me of an old book, which was appropriate for its location. The eyes that were carved into the center of the stone were the same as in Tenino, and I could see writing below them. The scrollwork seemed incredibly familiar to me, but I couldn't remember where I had seen it.

As we dusted off the stone, the patterns started to glow. However, before it reached its brightest intensity, all of the decorations except for a single sentence began to dim. The words were written in flowing, cursive English characters. It said: *Tantum musicorum modo aperiam.*

"Is it Latin?" I asked.

"Yes, I believe so." Hawkins responded. "If I am not mistaken, it reads, 'Only the musical instrument will open the way.' Literally translated of course."

What did this mean? I thought furiously as I stared at the tablet. It hit me where I had seen the scrollwork before. "Hawkins, it's your violin! The scrollwork on your violin looks the same as the scrollwork on the stone. I'll bet your violin is the instrument it means," I said excitedly.

"I don't know, Collins, it doesn't seem plausible."

"Sure it is! You said yourself that your violin is old, unique— and you didn't know where it originated or who owned it before. It has to be it! Come on, it's at least worth a try."

"Very well. I'll go and get it. You stay here."

Hawkins turned, hurried off down the lane, and was quickly out of my sight. As directed, I stayed with the tablet. Hawkins returned with his violin an hour later.

"What took so long?" I asked.

"I ran into our friend Inspector Nelson on the way. He is usually a taciturn fellow, but he has an uncanny ability to sense when one is in a hurry. It is then that he becomes most eloquent."

"I see. Can we hurry, please?"

"Here is my violin. Now what?" He brandished his unusual violin. "Good heavens!" As he spoke, he had been walking closer to the tablet, and the scrollwork on his violin had started glowing.

The violin is quite dark, but when the lines and details began to glow with an odd bluish hue it looked black. Hawkins turned the instrument over in his hands with a look of awe, and

I could see the familiar eye symbol on the back. There were no words below it, though. We looked at the stone and saw that it had changed in the presence of the violin.

"Hawkins, look!" I said, pointing at the tablet.

The tablet now held the outline of a violin. It was the same bluish hue as the inscriptions and pulsated slowly, like a beacon of sorts.

"It seems you were right, after all," Hawkins said. He knelt and placed the violin on the tablet.

To my astonishment, the stone expanded and the violin sank into its marble depths, lost to view.

"My violin!" Hawkins exclaimed. He reached out his hand to retrieve the instrument, but I grabbed his wrist to stop him. The tablet was glowing brightly, and the sentence had shrunk to a single word: Abierto

"It means 'open' in Spanish. This tablet is multilingual," I said quietly.

The word appeared and then disappeared with a similar effect. A row of various icons took its place. Each icon consisted of a small square with a symbol in the middle. All of the symbols were different, and there were few that I recognized.

"Whoa! This didn't happen in Tenino!" I exclaimed.

"Perhaps these symbols represent various places we can travel," Hawkins said.

"That makes sense. Should we try one and see what happens?"

"There is the letter A here, maybe it stands for a place of origin of some sort."

"Ok, let's try it."

"Collins, wait!"

I touched the icon, and the tablet lit up dramatically before knocking us unconscious with a final burst.

✳ CHAPTER XIX

HAWKINS AND I REGAINED consciousness simultaneously. I felt disoriented at first, but the feeling soon passed. Hawkins, however, wasn't so fortunate and was dizzy for a few minutes before he recovered. We were then able to study our surroundings.

The room we were in—for it was indeed a room—was peculiar. It was circular with a diameter of about eighteen feet. The walls and floor were both constructed of a strange material that I had never seen before and mostly unadorned. At one end of the room there was a pair of doors that had no handle and opposite them was another tablet. This tablet was glowing, and the decorations on it were clock-like. There was no furniture in the room.

There were no lights in the room, but light seemed to emanate from the walls themselves. In fact, as I studied the walls, I noticed that they seemed to be transparent in a way, and yet not. It sort of reminded me of a blown-glass sphere that has a light shining through it. The floor was similar, but whereas the walls were a whitish-red, the floor was black. The doors at the far end of the room were more like water in both color and appearance. Their surface seemed to be moving, though they felt solid when I touched them. We tried the doors, but they wouldn't open.

"You know, this is like something straight out of a sci-fi movie," I said. "I wonder if we'll be trapped in here forever."

"Have you noticed that time doesn't seem to be moving at all? I have no sense of passing moments, and the feeling of perpetually aging is gone," Hawkins responded.

"Whoa, you're right."

When a person is born, he immediately begins to die. This process is very slow for the majority of individuals, and we generally call it aging so it seems less gruesome to the general public. I had never been conscious of the fact I was aging continually until the sensation was gone, and it gave me a sense of freedom. It is almost like when there is a low sound nearby, and you don't really notice it until it is gone.

"Do you think we should check out that tablet over there? Maybe we can get back." I moved toward the stone, when there was a noise behind me. I turned around and saw that the doors had vanished, revealing a light beyond. More from curiosity than anything else, Hawkins and I walked into the next room.

This room was by far the oddest sight I had ever seen in my life. From left to right it was about as far across as London bridge is long, but it seemed to stretch forever in the other direction. The walls also were immense in height, and they appeared to consist of a continuous and well-stocked bookshelf. The floor of the room was solid and green, like turf, and crammed full of black desks. At each desk there sat a person who wrote furiously in a book of some sort, and beside him stood another person, who seemed to be a page. When a book had been filled, the page would give the person another book and take the filled one to the bookshelf. Any page that left a desk was immediately replaced by another. The room was in constant motion.

As soon as Hawkins and I went through the doorway, the door itself reappeared with a motion not unlike a glass being filled. There were several other doors lined up alongside it that also had the appearance of water, but each had a different color.

There were no lights in this room either, although it was bright. The light seemed to come from the beings themselves who gave off a golden hue.

"Do you suppose they ever stop writing?" Hawkins asked. His voice seemed strangely loud, for the room was very quiet. None of its occupants seemed to notice us. I was about to respond to his remark, when a large being appeared directly in front of us.

How this being appeared without our notice is beyond me, but it was different than all of the others. The people at the desks appeared to be humans, but this one was clearly not of our race. Its face was smooth with a complexion that made me think of a lightening bolt, and angular, it had catlike features. The piercing eyes didn't seem to have color. There was nothing harsh in this being's gaze but only a soft sense of wonder. Its ears were hidden beneath its long, straight, white hair. Although I was tall, I had to look up to see its face. It was difficult to discern any clothing, but the being seemed to be clothed in light itself, as odd as it sounds. There was nothing in this creature's appearance to hint at gender, but when it finally spoke, its voice had a hint of masculinity in it, so I decided to think of it as a male.

"Dr. Andrew Michael Collins and William Scott Jeremiah Hawkins," he said. His voice was powerful like when thunder is building up and yet soft like a breeze through a patch of grass.

"Are you God?" I stammered without thinking. The being smiled, which oddly put me at ease.

"No, I am Custos, the Guardian. I have been charged with the task of keeping history and protecting the timeline. The room you see before you is where the history of every being on earth is being written. Every action you make and thought you think is recorded in a book. When that book is full, it is placed on a shelf beside the other books of your history."

"But why?" I asked. "There must be a better way of doing it."

"There are several, but this way is preferred. The beings you see before you are writers of a sort. Some have volunteered to write forever, and others are being punished. They will record the history of the world until it is destroyed, and then they will begin anew with the history of the new Earth."

"There is a sort of symbolism to it all," Hawkins pointed out. I shuddered to think of an eternity of writing.

"This is all very fascinating, but I don't follow how we got here or what the tablet have to do with it."

"The tablets, as you call them, form a network that can take an individual anywhere in time and place. Humans were never meant to use them, and it is fortunate that you ended up here and not somewhere else."

"Why were the tablets created?" Hawkins asked.

"One of my kindred was banished many thousands of years ago by your standards. He was outraged by this humiliation and retaliated by attempting to destroy the fabric of time. He nearly succeeded, but was stopped. The damage was extensive and more than I can repair. My helpers, as you might think of them, are humans like yourselves and yet very different. They cannot move through time and space as I can, so I created the tablets for them. They were given the knowledge for operating the network. Thus, they were able to move through time and the earth, and the timeline was repaired."

As he talked, Custos led us out of the writing room and into a different room. This room was somewhat ovular, dark, and blue. The ceiling and floor were pulled toward each other in the center, which made the ceiling seem lower than it actually was. Where the two met, there was a transparent screen. Custos went to it and tapped it gently. The screen sprung to life and lit up with many rows of icons. Custos tapped one of these, and a map of the earth with red dots connected by lines appeared.

"This is all very incredible," Hawkins said as he looked around him in open wonder.

"It must seem so to you, Jeremy Hawkins. You have not been exposed to the technology that Dr. Collins has, and yet he has only witnessed what other men dream of. I do not expect you to comprehend all that you see, for you were not meant to, but I will do my best to satisfy your curiosity. Now then," he turned to the map on the screen, "This is a map of earth with the network of tablets displayed on it. Their operation is abstruse and complex and I would require many of your years to explain it all. Even then, you would not understand fully."

"You keep saying 'your time'; don't you guys use the same clock?" I asked.

"No, we exist outside of time, and you do also as long as you remain here."

"How long are we to remain here?" asked Hawkins.

"There is no time; therefore, you would not remain for long or short. You are simply here, and when you leave you will no longer be here. There is no now or later."

"That doesn't make any sense," I said.

"It is only confusing because you are limited by the concept of time. Come with me." Custos led us through another door that reminded me of cherry Kool-Aid and into a strange room. It was as if we were merely standing in emptiness, and I was suddenly aware of the passage of time again.

"What is this place?"

"This area is affected by time and will be easier for you to comprehend. We must discuss why you are here."

"It was kind of by accident," I began.

"You were trying to change the past, Dr. Collins."

I suddenly felt like I was being accused of something. "Yes, I guess I was."

"There is no guessing. Were you or were you not attempting to re-write the past?"

"I was."

Custos seemed to grow and shrink as we spoke. Although his voice remained soft, it reverberated off the nothingness with a terrifying harshness. "Do you also acknowledge that you have been knowingly living in the wrong time period for one year, two months, and twenty days?"

"Well, I tried to get back."

"Do you acknowledge this?"

"Yes."

"When you did make it back to your own time period, you then sought a means back to the wrong time period. Correct?"

"Yes."

"Then, Dr. Andrew Michael Collins, you are guilty of willfully contaminating the timeline with your unauthorized presence in the wrong century."

"But it wasn't his fault!" Hawkins protested.

"Silence, Jeremy Hawkins, you do not have license to speak."

Hawkins bowed his head, and took a step backwards. Custos turned back to me. "Dr. Collins, do you believe that there is a reason for everything?"

"What?" I was a little taken aback by this question, for it seemed out of place.

"Please answer the question."

"Yes, I guess so. I mean, yes, I do."

"Then you believe that your presence in the 19th century was not a mere chance event, but that you were there for a reason?"

"I hadn't really thought of it that way before."

"Then you must think of it now."

"I believe I was there for a reason."

"Very well. Why do you seek to change the past?"

"Because a lot of things happened to a lot of people, and none of it was good."

"But if everything happens for a reason, why should you not let time proceed as it will? Who are you to say it is for the better?"

"I don't pretend to be God, that's way out of my league. But I just know that this is not how things are supposed to be."

"So your actions are based off a hunch."

"No. Well, yes I guess they are. But it's not just a hunch."

"Do you realize the seriousness of what you are proposing to accomplish, Dr. Collins? By attempting to change what has already occurred, you could inadvertently destroy the very fabric of the space time continuum and all because of your hunch. Are you still resolute?"

"You said 'could.' So that means it is possible that I won't be responsible for the destruction of the universe?"

"You have not answered my question."

"Since you imply that there is a chance the world won't be destroyed, then yes, I am still resolute."

"Your selfishness is appalling! You would risk the lives of millions just to save a couple of your friends who are able to live out their lives in relative comfort?"

"There are worse things than death, and I know for a fact at least one of my friends faces a fate worse than death if he goes on living as he is. He is a broken man, and I know he cannot stand it. You write history and control time and what not, surely you must see this?"

"The suffering of one individual is not enough to justify the destruction of an entire world."

"The possible destruction of an entire world; and if you could keep your best friend from a life of suffering, wouldn't you?"

"You propose to return to a point prior to the moment when Professor Stephen Elliot Davies murdered you and your wife in order to prevent that event from occurring, correct?"

"Yes."

"Is this to save your wife or to prevent the consequences of this event from occurring?"

"Both."

"Please elaborate."

"By saving my wife, I think it would keep the consequences of her death from happening. Besides, it is my fault that she died. I mean, if I hadn't shown up in the 19th century, it is likely that none of this would have happened."

"Then your only alternative is to return to your proper century, and I will reset the past so that it will be as if you never went to London."

"What? No! Please, you can't do that to me!"

"But it is clearly the best way."

"Oh please! You can't do that!" I fell on my knees and clasped my hands together in supplication. "The 19th century is the best thing that's ever happened to me. I've learned so much and made true friends. For the first time in my life, I belonged, and you have no idea what a wonderful feeling it is to belong! You can't take me away, it would be just cruel!"

"I will give you a choice. You may return to your proper timeline when the timeline will be reset, or you may stay in 19th-century London, such as it was when you left. If you choose the former option, you will have accomplished something, but if the latter, your trip will have been in vain."

A wave of dismay washed over me as I realized that either way I would be separated from my loved one. If I chose the latter option, though, I would be where I belonged, but it would be in the London that was a nightmare. There was a chance I could adjust to this new London, but my goal of saving my wife would've been in vain. If I chose the former, everything would be fine for everyone else, but I would be separated from them all.

"These are my only options?"

"Yes. You must choose now."

"Then I'll go with the first choice."

"And why is that, Doctor Collins?"

Somehow, that question annoyed me, but I answered it anyway. "If I choose that option, I know that my wife will be alive and well. I will not have been responsible for her death, and I won't have to live with that knowledge."

"But you will be abandoning the people whom you named your only true friends."

"Well, maybe they would be better off without me in the end anyway."

"You would be forced to live in an era where you don't fit in. Are you sure you are willing to live in such a place? A moment ago you were begging me not to take you away from London."

"If it will save my friends and set things right, I will live even in hell if I have to. It's not just about me and what will make me happy."

"Dr. Collins, you have answered wisely."

"Huh?"

"You have proven that you do not have your own interests at heart but that you strive to accomplish a goal that will benefit all. Therefore, I will grant your request and give you a chance to repair the past. However, in return there is something you must do for me, as a final test of your character."

"Thank you! I'll do it! Whatever it is, I'll do it!"

"Do not be so hasty, doctor, for the outcome may not be in your favor. I want you to shut down the network of tablets for me."

"Ok, I can do that if you tell me how."

"Are you certain that you are willing to do this? If you fail in your attempt to fix the past, you will be forced to live with the consequences of your failure."

"At least I will have tried. I'll do it."

"Very well, Dr. Collins, here is what you must do. I will give you a chessboard, and you will return to the tablet in London. You must place the chessboard over the tablet, and it will be absorbed as the violin was. After this, your friend must play a game of chess."

I chuckled, thinking how easy this would be and looked over at Hawkins to see his reaction. When I looked at him, I was surprised to see that he looked like a statue. His eyes were fixed on a point just beyond where I was, and he appeared out of focus as well.

"Hawkins?" I said, concerned for my friend.

"Do not be alarmed. I have placed him in an area where time moves at a different rate. He is not aware of our conversation or the passage of time and will suffer no ill effects." I shuddered at the power of this being that could place people in different time zones without my notice.

"Why don't you want him to hear what we are saying?"

"It is for your ears alone."

"Oh. He has to play a game of chess? Against who?"

"His opponent will be the tablet itself."

"So it's like playing against the computer."

"If you wish, you may think of it in that sense. The game will be an easy one for your friend to win, and therefore he must strive to lose this game."

"To lose? But he's never lost a game! There's no way he'll agree to that."

"You must convince him."

"But why does he have to lose? What's the point of that?"

"Your friend is more significant than both of you realize, and it is fortunate for you that he was the person you ran into. When you unearthed the London tablet, you found that the key to arriving here was in the chess master's violin, but your key to return will be in the chess master himself. Do you understand?"

"Not entirely. You didn't really answer my question."

"It is the only answer I can give you. Do you understand what you must do?"

"I think so. Get Hawkins to lose a game of chess to the tablet, right?"

"Precisely. Once the game has been played, the timeline will revert so that you will have your second chance, and the tablets will be shut down. Be aware doctor that you will not return to the 21st century should you be fatally wounded or killed. You are no longer invincible."

"Ok, I get it—don't die."

"Yes. I will return the two of you to London now. I have also frozen time around the tablet so that you will not be disturbed. Good luck, doctor."

"Wait, what happens if Hawkins wins the game?"

"You will be tried for your crimes against the timeline and punished accordingly, as will your friend."

"What would the punishment be? Death?"

"Dr. Collins, there are worse things than death. Goodbye."

All of a sudden, the mysterious dark room was gone along with its occupant, and Hawkins and I were standing on the dirt lane in London once more, with a glass chessboard in the dust between us.

CHAPTER XX

LOOKED AT THE WORLD AROUND ME for a moment as I slowly came back to my senses. It was such a jolt to return to the normal world after the amazing sights I had seen. I remembered my mission, though, and turned to my dazed companion.

"Hawkins!" I half shouted.

He looked at me vacantly. "Yes?"

"Ok, so Custos put you in this alternate timeline thingy so you couldn't hear our conversation, and it was really weird. But anyway, he gave me some instructions, ok?"

"That explains quite a bit."

"Yeah. So here's what we've got to do. He's going to let me change history, but we've got to shut down the tablets first."

"How, pray tell, are we to accomplish this?"

"I'm getting to that. For whatever reason, I can't shut them down. It has to be you. It's something having to do with fate, destiny, and the end of the world. Anyway, all it involves a chess game."

"A chess game? That doesn't seem difficult."

"Yeah, but there's a catch. You have to play against the tablet itself—"

"Strange, but no doubt doable."

"—and you have to lose."

He stood absolutely still for a moment with a blank expression, and I dreaded his answer.

"Fine. I will do it."

"Really?"

"No! Absolutely not! It is quite out of the question."

I sighed, wishing that my friend had a different temperament. "You have to do it! People's lives are at stake here! Come on, we've made it this far, don't quit now. I can't do it without you."

He stared at me harshly, and I put on my most pathetic and pleading face. He finally relented.

"Alright! I will do it."

"Good! Oh, by the way, the tablet will try to make you win, so you will have to strive to lose."

"Of course, it will," he said, throwing his hands in the air with exasperation. "How could I possibly expect anything different? Let me guess. If I fail, we all die. Correct?"

"I think so."

"Excellent."

I smiled slightly at his sarcasm and picked the chessboard out of the dirt by my feet. It had apparently arrived with us, although I hadn't noticed it at first. I set the chessboard on the tablet, and it was absorbed as the violin had been. The two of them merged to become a new and well-lit playing board. The chess pieces faded into existence, and the game was set.

"Good luck," I said.

"It is not luck that will help me now," Hawkins replied. He took his place on the side of the board where the white pieces were set up and rubbed his hands together while considering his first move. He started by moving his pawn to square D4, and the game that followed this move was no doubt the most singular to take place in chess history. In order for either side to win, the other actually had to lose. This meant that they were playing the game backwards or contrary to the conventional method. Even though I was not well versed in the nuances of chess, I was able to see obvious means of checkmate that each side passed up. Key pieces were placed so that they could easily be snatched, but neither side took the bait. Hawkins even moved his king into the center of the chessboard to aid his opponent, but twenty moves into the game, both sides still had all of their pieces.

True to Custos' word, time did not seem to pass as the chess game took place. My heart leapt within me when Hawkins accidentally put his opponent in check once, but he was able to avoid doing so again. Slowly, and with much trial, Hawkins boxed his own king in on all but one side. The next part of his strategy was to trick his opponent into moving a piece into the position that would checkmate Hawkins' king. He accomplished this by placing his opponent's king in check but not before making sure that the only means of alleviating the threat was to conquer Hawkins' attacking piece. When the brain behind the tablet removed the threat against his king, Hawkins' king was effectively blocked from making any legal moves.

Hawkins let out an exclamation of relief and collapsed backwards exhausted. The word checkmate lit up the chessboard, and the chess pieces disappeared. The surface of the tablet became slightly muddled for a moment and started glowing brightly. I turned to Hawkins and pulled him to his feet.

"Good job! That was awesome!" I exclaimed.

"Do you hear that?"

"Hear what?"

I heard a low humming sound and traced it to the tablet itself. There was a vortex of light surrounding the stone, and it was revolving lazily around in a circle while producing the sound. As the vortex spun faster, the noise grew higher pitched and more intense. A great wind came up, and I felt like I was being pulled toward the tablet. It wasn't until I noticed that I couldn't move no matter what I tried that I panicked.

"Hawkins!" I shouted over the noise. "I can't move!"

He was right next to me, but he looked a mile away, and I couldn't make out what he said when he shouted. The scenery around us had blurred into a shapeless mass of white light, and it too was revolving around us. I looked down at my feet. I seemed to be suspended in mid-air. When I looked back up, Hawkins was gone.

"Hawkins! No!"

The sound and light grew in intensity to the point that I could not shut either of them out. Just when I felt I could no longer stand it, the noise and light disappeared, as did the feeling of being dragged forward.

I opened my eyes tentatively. To my inestimable joy, I recognized my surroundings immediately. I was standing in the entryway of 37c Montague Street, and I was hugging Mrs. Montgomery. For a moment I couldn't remember what day it was, but I then realized that it was my wedding day, and I was hugging my former landlady goodbye. I pulled Mrs. Montgomery away from me and held her at arm's length for a moment so I could see her face. It was exactly as I had remembered it and even showed the evidence that she had been crying.

"Doctor?" She asked, looking up at me with a worried expression.

"Oh, Mrs. Montgomery, I'm so glad you're not dead!" I exclaimed. Tears of joy streamed down my face, and I hugged her tightly.

"I'm certainly glad to be alive also, Dr. Collins," she said in confusion.

It was a few moments before I could draw myself away, and she patted my arm with a smile. I smiled back and noticed the figure behind her. My heart leapt into my throat when I saw Agatha standing there, smiling sweetly. It took all of my self-control to keep me from rushing to her, for I knew it would be seen as strange. Instead, I let out a sort of choked gurgle and burst into tears.

"Oh darling, I had no idea you would be so affected," she said sympathetically. Her voice was like balm to my tortured heart, and I drank in the sight of her greedily.

"I'm so sorry, guys," I gasped between sobs. "Guess I'm a little emotional right now."

"There, there, now, it'll be alright." She approached me and embraced me lovingly until I finally stopped crying.

"You'll be alright now, doctor?" Mrs. Montgomery asked.

I blew my nose loudly and wiped my eyes with my handkerchief. "Yeah, I'm fine now." A smile crept over my face. "You two have never looked lovelier!"

"Well, aren't you a sweet gentleman," Agatha said. "We have to leave soon, dear, or we will miss our train." She headed for the door, and I suddenly remembered why I was here.

"Hawkins! I forgot about him! I'll be back in a minute."

"But Andrew—"

I didn't hear a word she said to me, as I realized that I didn't have much time. I dashed up the stairs as quickly as I could and burst into the sitting room, pausing in a moment of déjà vu. Hawkins was standing with his back to me, chewing on his pipe just as he had last time. He turned around when I entered and smiled with an amused expression.

"I did not expect to see you back so soon, did you forget something?" he said nonchalantly. I was overjoyed to see that this was definitely not the broken Hawkins I had just convinced to lose a chess game. His eyes sparkled just as I remembered. It seemed a lifetime since I had seen him display his masterful ways—so much had happened in the interval.

"Hawkins! We need to talk!" I said urgently.

"My dear fellow, what is it?"

"We don't have as much time as I had hoped, so I'll explain quickly. You remember when I first came here and you believed my story even though it was completely outrageous? Well, I need you to trust me again, ok?"

"Please calm yourself and tell me exactly what is going on."

"You know how you always tell me that nothing's impossible? Well, I've been to the future. Well no not the future. It was kind of the future, but hopefully it won't happen now, so it's kind of an alternate timeline I guess."

"Collins, you aren't making any sense."

"Davies is going to kidnap Agatha and me when we get to the train station today."

"Collins, Davies is safely ensconced on the Andaman Islands—"

"No, he escaped. I don't know how, but he did, and he's bent on revenge, and he's going to ruin everything."

"How could you possibly know—"

"Look, he shot me in the head and I died, but not really. I ended up in the 21st century again and apparently if I die here I go back there, but not anymore since we shut down the tablets. Anyway, so I was there a few weeks, and then the wood smoke triggered a flashback, which made me realize that I belong here. So I came back here, but everyone was either dead or as good as, so I got you to help me even though you were depressed and stuff. We got to this alternate dimension thing, and Custos told me I could change time, but I had to shut down the tablets to do it. I guess we succeeded since I'm here and you don't remember any of this. Anyway that's how I'm here."

"Your grammar certainly hasn't improved in the interval."

"Hawkins! This is not a good time for criticism. I need your help!"

"Calm yourself, Collins, I already have a plan."

"Good!"

I DESCENDED THE STAIRCASE feeling a little more reassured but not too much calmer. Mrs. Montgomery and Agatha were waiting for me, and I relived my tearful final goodbye with Mrs. Montgomery. Agatha and I exited the house. Before we climbed into the carriage, I pulled her close, kissed her, and held on to her with all my might, remembering how she had been so quickly taken from me before.

"Andrew, are you well? You've been acting odd." Agatha asked, interrupting my troubled thoughts.

"I've wanted to do that for a long time."

She smiled quizzically, and we climbed into the carriage. Déjà vu once again haunted me as we pulled away from 37c. Mrs.

Montgomery was even waving at us from the bottom step like last time. My mind turned from this odd feeling, and I tapped my fingers nervously against my leg. Hawkins hadn't told me what his plan was, but I silently prayed that it would work.

"Are you sure you're not ill?" Agatha asked.

"How could I ever be sick when I'm with you?" I answerd.

She smiled, and I put my arm around her shoulders, holding her close until we arrived at the station.

Just like my previous experience, the train platform was practically deserted, and we were the only two people who stood waiting for the train, which was again running horribly late. I looked around the empty platform nervously but saw nothing suspicious. Agatha squeezed my hand, and I jumped.

"Why Andrew, you're as nervous as a cat!" she exclaimed.

I was about to respond, but in terror I felt the nose of gun dig into my back. A darkly dressed figure appeared behind Agatha, and a voice told us to keep quiet. I had been too startled last time to recognize the voice as that of Davies himself, and I guessed that Billy was the figure who captured Agatha. Davies started to lead us off, but a voice rang out authoritatively through the silence and held him in place. It was Hawkins.

"Drop your gun, Stephen. We don't want any violence now, do we?"

I heard Davies mutter a curse against Hawkins, and he maneuvered so that I was between the two of them.

"How the devil did you come to be here? Never mind, it matters not. I shall still have my revenge." He held his gun against the side of my head. "Now then, Jeremy, why don't you just throw your gun over this way? It would be unfortunate if your friend were to meet his end so soon."

Hawkins hesitated but then tossed his gun toward us. It came up a few feet short and landed on the pavement heavily.

"Excellent. Now raise your hands over your head so that I can see them. Very nice. If you so much as twitch, I will have no compunction in blowing your friend's brains across the platform." He turned toward his young partner in crime. "Billy, take the lady to the carriage and wait for me there."

Billy complied and roughly dragged Agatha toward the exit. She looked at me helplessly, and anger welled up inside of me. I looked at Hawkins, and his own face went pale as he read my expression. He shook his head slightly, and mouthed the word "no" just so I could see it. I nodded grimly as if to say "oh yes, I'm going to do it" and then made my move.

The events that occurred next moved in slow motion but lasted a mere few seconds. I elbowed Davies in the face with my left elbow and grabbed at the gun with my right hand. I managed to grab his wrist, and we struggled. At the same moment that I attacked Davies, Hawkins pulled out a whistle and blew it while he dived for his gun. I heard the sound of running feet. A moment after my struggle began, Davies threw me to the ground and pointed his gun level with my forehead. A gunshot echoed through the still air. Davies doubled over with his hand on his chest, dropping his gun at the same time. Blood seeped from beneath his hand, and he was dead within a matter of seconds.

I looked at Hawkins, but he hadn't reached his gun yet. Confused, I looked up at the group of constables led by Inspector Nelson and Thomas Blessington who had just arrived on the scene, but none of them had their guns out.

"Who shot him?" I asked.

We all turned simultaneously and looked at Agatha. She was standing with her feet wide apart, holding a smoking revolver in both of her trembling hands. The look on her face was one of pride and horror, and much of her hair had escaped its bun. Billy, the owner of the revolver, was lying on the ground unconscious.

"Aggie!" I said in astonishment.

She jumped and relaxed her rigid posture a little. "Oh dear," she said and promptly fainted.

Hawkins and I exchanged a glance, and I clambered to my feet before rushing over to my unconscious wife. I could hear the three of them talking as I hurried over.

"Inspector Nelson, I see you had my telegram. Thank you for responding so promptly to my note," Hawkins said graciously to the scowling Inspector.

"It was marked urgent, Mr. Hawkins."

"Quite so. Ah, Mr. Blessington! Always a pleasure, sir."

Blessington laughed heartily. "I hardly expected to see you two so soon or under such circumstances. You just can't keep out of trouble, can you?"

"I had no idea Davies had escaped. It is very lucky that we stopped him," said Inspector Nelson. "But how on earth did you know, Mr. Hawkins?"

"A little sparrow flapped into my sitting room and told me the whole story."

Inspector Nelson and Blessington weren't satisfied with Hawkins' answer, but I tuned out the rest of their conversation when I reached Agatha. I knelt next to her and propped her against my legs. She was regaining consciousness and I noticed that Billy had already been taken away.

"Darling, are you alright?" I asked softly. Her eyelids fluttered, and she looked up at me dazedly.

"Andrew? Did I kill him? Is he alright?"

"Well, you did get him, and I'm afraid he's beyond any aid."

She closed her eyes and sighed sadly. "Oh, Andrew, I didn't mean to kill him, but he was going to harm you. I couldn't let that happen. I was so afraid I would lose you."

"I know the feeling." I muttered under my breath. Then out loud, "It's ok, Aggie, I don't think there was anything we could do to help him anyway. Maybe death was the best thing for him."

"Maybe."

She quickly recovered, and we joined the group of men who appeared to have settled their differences. Davies' body was being carried away as we approached, and Inspector Nelson was just recording a few notes in his notebook.

"It appears to be a case of self-defense," he was saying as we approached. "Davies was never very stable anyway, so I believe he simply suffered a complete leave of his senses, and you were justified in your actions."

"Thank you, Inspector Nelson." Hawkins replied.

"I would still like to know how you knew what Davies was going to do," Blessington said.

"My dear Mr. Blessington, even I have secrets I must keep."

"I suppose we can allow one secret," Nelson said. "Come, Blessington. We have work to do."

"Very good, sir. Good day, gentlemen, my lady." Blessington, Nelson, and their group of constables evacuated the station.

"It looks like your plan worked out pretty well," I observed. "What was it, anyway?"

"It was quite simple. I left the house nearly at the same time you did and quickly dispatched an urgent telegram to both Nelson and Blessington. I requested them to arrive here with a group of constables as quickly as they could. After this was finished, I hastened to the train station by means of a shortcut. Even so, I arrived after you had been here some time. I was fortunate in my timing though as you saw, and I hoped to stall Davies long enough for the Inspector and his men to arrive. The rest you know. You made an extremely foolish move, the Inspector and his men came running at my whistle, and dear Aggie was the heroine of the day."

"It wasn't that foolish." I said.

"You could have been killed, and would have been if it weren't for the marksmanship of your bride."

"Yeah, you're right." We stood silent for a moment, and I could hear our train approaching. I would have to say goodbye to Hawkins. I wasn't looking forward to reliving that. "I think that's our train."

"So it would seem," Hawkins replied.

"I wonder why it is so late," Agatha said.

"Merely because the two of you were quite earlier than you thought," Hawkins announced.

"What do you mean?" I asked.

"Precisely what I said. I recently discovered that the clock at our lodgings is quite fast. It seems as though someone has been winding it far too often."

"Oh."

"It is your own fault. I did tell you to find a reliable pocket watch."

"Wait, then how did Davies know to expect us?"

"He is not an imbecile, and it is likely that he was spying on us for quite some time."

"Ah."

The train rumbled up to the platform with a bellow of steam and sighed with relief as it came to a halt. A flood of humanity disembarked from within the great beast, and a corresponding flood boarded to refill its seats. Agatha kissed her brother on the cheek to bid him goodbye and then made her way through the flood to our compartment.

"Take good care of her, Collins. She is a remarkable woman," Hawkins said.

"Don't worry, I will. So, I'm going to, uh, well, I'm going to miss you. Thanks for everything."

"It is I who should be thanking you, for it seems as though you have saved my life many times." He paused and pulled a small parcel out of his pocket. "No English gentleman should be without one of these, and I hope you will accept it as a small token of my gratitude."

I opened the small parcel and discovered a beautiful silver pocket watch inside complete with a chain. My initials were engraved on the front cover and on the inside of the lid was an engraving of a pair of eyes—identical to those on the tablets. I looked up quickly, but Hawkins was gone. I thought I could pick him out near the exit, but there were so many people that I couldn't be sure. I put the watch into my waistcoat pocket and looped the chain through a buttonhole. It was an item I would treasure for the rest of my life.

"To Paris, my husband," Agatha said when I had joined her on the train.

"Let's get going, my dearest. We have our entire lives ahead of us now."

"You still haven't told me why you were so agitated earlier," she stated as she leaned her head on my arm.

"Well, here's what happened—"

I told her the entire story that would eventually give birth to a popular, albeit fictional, legend among the later generations of my family. They always referred to it as the Tale of the Chess Master, and it is in honor of that legend that I name this story The Chess Master's Violin, which contains the facts surrounding my arrival in London. Hawkins was averse to having this account published, and it has taken a bit of coercion to obtain his permission. My wife had much to do with it, and I am grateful for all of her assistance, which has been quite invaluable.

Following a lengthy and absolutely heavenly honeymoon in the romantic city of Paris, Agatha and I returned to Surrey so that I could fill my role as a country squire. I must admit that I fill this role rather well, and my wife and I are happy. Hawkins comes up now and then to visit us and even takes a few random holidays on the estate. I have always wondered what Custos meant when he told me that Hawkins' role was scarcely realized, but I suppose all will be revealed in the fullness of time. Until then, I will live out my days with the happy knowledge that I defied and rendered useless the word impossible, and I did it with the help of my best friend, Livesey Hawkins.

THE END

CPSIA information can be obtained at www.ICGtesting.com
Printed in the USA
BVOW070526250612

293485BV00001B/12/P